THE SANIBEL SUNSET DETECTIVE SAVES THE WORLD

Also by Ron Base

Fiction

Matinee Idol
Foreign Object
Splendido
Magic Man
The Strange
The Sanibel Sunset Detective
The Sanibel Sunset Detective Returns
Another Sanibel Sunset Detective
The Two Sanibel Sunset Detectives
The Hound of the Sanibel Sunset Detective
The Confidence Man
The Four Wives of the Sanibel Sunset Detective
The Escarpment
The Sanibel Sunset Detective Goes to London
Heart of the Sanibel Sunset Detective
The Dame with the Sanibel Sunset Detective
The Mill Pond
I, The Sanibel Sunset Detective
Main Street, Milton
Bring Me the Head of the Sanibel Sunset Detective
The Hidden Quarry
The Devil and the Sanibel Sunset Detective

Dark Edge Novellas

The White Island
The Secret Stones

Non-fiction

The Movies of the Eighties (with David Haslam)
If the Other Guy Isn't Jack Nicholson, I've Got the Part
Marquee Guide to Movies on Video
Cuba Portrait of an Island (with Donald Nausbaum)

www.ronbase.com
Contact Ron at
ronbase@ronbase.com

THE
SANIBEL SUNSET
DETECTIVE
SAVES THE
WORLD

RON BASE

West-End
Books

Library and Archives Canada Cataloguing in Publication

Title: The Sanibel sunset detective saves the world / Ron Base.
Names: Base, Ron, author.
Identifiers: Canadiana 20210273933 | ISBN 9781990058011 (softcover)
Classification: LCC PS8553.A784 S28 2021 | DDC C813/.54—dc23

Publisher's Note: This is a work of fiction. Names, characters,
places, and incidents either are products of the author's imagination
or are used fictitiously. Any resemblance to actual persons,
events, or locales is entirely coincidental.

West-End Books
133 Mill St.
Milton, Ontario
L9T 1S1

Text design and electronic formatting: Ric Base
Cover design and coordination: Jennifer Smith
Sanibel-Captiva map: Ann Kornuta
Cover photo: ConceptCafe

"Nothing in the world can surprise me now. For Zeus, the father of the Olympian, has turned the midday into black night by shielding light from the blossoming Sun, and now dark terror hangs over mankind. Anything may happen."

7th Century Greek poet Archilochus witnessing a solar eclipse

On August 21, more than seven million people from across the globe are predicted to converge on Florida as the first total eclipse since 1917 to cross the North American continent from ocean to ocean takes place. Millions are expected to witness the once-in-a-lifetime event. Various evangelical groups across the US have already heralded the eclipse as a sign of impending apocalypse, that it will spark the beginning of the so-called Tribulation, a period in which the world's population will be destroyed.

2021 AP News Report

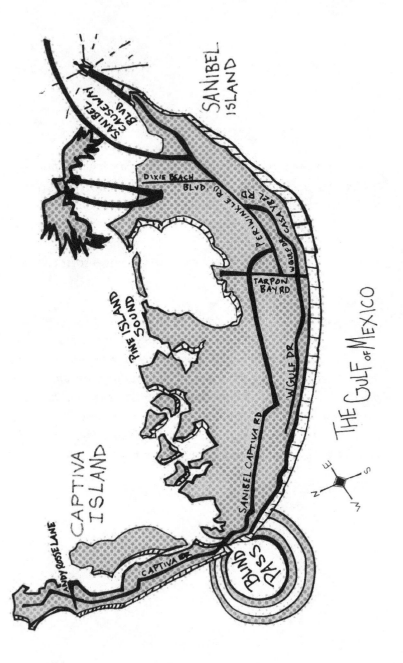

1

At 17:30 hours, during the time when a video recording might have gone a long way toward confirming what actually happened, the lights and camera went out inside Rebecca 'Becky' McPhee's spheroidal dome helmet.

This happened approximately one hour after she exited the International Space Station's Quest Airlock. She was wearing a hybrid space suit consisting of both hard-shell parts and fabric. Her mission was to replace the aging nickel-hydrogen batteries for one of the two power channels on the far starboard truss of the space station with the new lithium-ion batteries that had recently arrived on board a Japanese cargo spacecraft.

A Navy SEAL in her previous professional life who had served in both Iraq and Afghanistan, this was Astronaut McPhee's first extravehicular activity (EVA). Until now, she'd had mixed feelings about her experience aboard the ISS. Like most rookie astronauts, she delighted in the feeling of weightlessness that was the hallmark of life in the space station. Sleeping peacefully on the ceiling? Nothing like it on earth, that was for sure. Passing the ketchup? You simply floated it across the table.

But if discovering the possibilities of weightlessness was the fun part for a rookie, space sickness, as it was called, was no fun at all. For Becky, that meant reoccurring bouts of gut-wrenching nausea as her body fought to adjust to an alien environment it didn't like.

The size of a football field, the ISS was now over twenty years old and showing its age: a leak here, a backed-up toilet there, and don't forget the necessity to maneuver the spacecraft around every so often in order to dodge a meteor or a stray piece of space debris.

Now the problem was the loss of her camera and lights. But that's what it was all about, wasn't it—adapting to the unforeseen, fixing what could be quickly fixed and then getting on with it?

She checked with her counterpart, a handsome, good-natured Russian cosmonaut named Yuri Revin whom she liked a lot. Together they agreed Becky should proceed with the mission. If she finished installation of the new batteries ahead of schedule, then the plan still called for her to fill the allotted mission time with what was called a getahead task. In this instance, the designated getahead was cleaning and replacing glare filters on the NASA TV cameras which were supposed to have also been available to film her spacewalk.

As it turned out, Becky never got to perform that task and the glare filters malfunctioned, obscuring the events that soon unfolded.

All astronauts report that they are unprepared for the exhilarating, life-changing experience that is their first spacewalk, the kind of euphoria it induces, the dazzling feeling that comes from floating in space two-hundred-and-fifty miles above the earth. Up here, the third rock from the sun is borderless, shifting landmasses beneath white clouds, greener than green, the oceans bluer than blue.

No matter how much she had heard about it, no matter how many times others had described it, this experience was uniquely hers, breath-taking, moments she would treasure for the rest of her life. She thought of what she had gone through with the SEALs, the heart-pounding tension, the sense, no matter how hard she tried to ignore it, that at any moment she could be dead. The fact that she came out alive and more or less intact, constantly amazed her. Applying for the astronaut program had been a way of finally shaking off the specter of death. Now, floating so far above the earth, she felt restored, the past washed away. She had been made invincible, immortal, reaching for the heavens.

Hearing the Voice…

Becky was paused, overwhelmed by the deep emotions she was feeling, when she heard it. An indistinct murmur at first. Briefly, she thought her radio had been reactivated. But then she realized it wasn't her radio.

The murmur grew louder—a voice. Surrounding her. That was impossible, she told herself. She was floating in space for God's sake, a kid from Fort Myers, Florida on her first spacewalk, yes, but also a battle-hardened professional with all her wits about her and certainly not someone who heard voices.

But that's exactly what she was hearing…a *voice.*

The Voice grew louder and clearer, and dammit, she *was* hearing it, speaking directly to her. The Voice was somehow genderless, simply…a *voice.* Nothing like the sort of deep, basso profundo she heard in those 1950s Biblical movies that her father loved to inflict on her. But a—well, there was only one way to describe it—a *reasonable* voice.

Which made the words spoken all the more chilling, a conversational tone about… Oh, God, she thought.

The authoritative Voice of doom announcing the end of the world.

2

TEN DAYS BEFORE THE END OF THE WORLD

Tree Callister was working the keyboard on his laptop, navigating through the steps necessary to renew his State of Florida Private Investigator license when Rex Baxter carrying two lattes, entered their office at the back of the Cattle Dock Bait Company.

"Don't make any plans for the future," Rex announced. "It's all over. The world is coming to an end."

"So I hear," Tree said. "I'd better hurry up and get my license renewed."

"Here we are just recovering from a pandemic that's devastated the country, a controversial and divisive election, and now this," Rex groused as he placed one of the lattes on Tree's desk.

"The end of the world according to Florida's own Becky McPhee." Tree tore himself away from his computer screen and looked up at Rex.

"We have to take her seriously, I suppose," Rex said, settling into his chair. "After all, she's an astronaut as well as a former Navy SEAL who saw combat. She defies NASA, who apparently tried to keep her quiet, and holds a press conference to announce she heard a voice telling her that the world will come to an end at the next solar eclipse on the twenty first of August."

"You're right, that's only ten days away," Tree noted. "That's why I'm rushing to get this renewal finished."

"Becky sure has had an effect. Everyone freaks out, then she disappears, and everyone freaks out even more." Rex was shaking his head. "One more crisis this country must endure."

"You seem to be handling it pretty calmly," Tree noted.

"At my age, I'm not going to worry too much about the end of the world. For me, it will end soon enough, anyway. Besides, I got bigger things to be concerned about."

"Like what?" Tree asked.

"Like visiting the Barnes and Noble bookstore yesterday and not being able to find my book."

"It wasn't there?"

"The clerk said they had two copies. Said so on the computer. But do you think he could find them?"

"He couldn't?"

Rex shook his head. "As I suspected, the damned publisher has screwed up. The books aren't out there."

Rex's autobiography, *I Slept with Joan Crawford: Wild Tales of Nights in Hollywood* had recently been published by a small Florida-based publisher. Like authors the world over, Rex was not happy, beginning to discover that perhaps the greatest impediment to a successful book was the book's oblivious, uncaring publisher.

"It's like your agent told you, Rex. The publisher won't do much of anything. You have to get out there and sell it yourself."

Rex didn't appear to hear his friend or, if he did, he was choosing to ignore him. "What's more, I now find myself back serving you lattes every morning. I believe that's where we started out down here."

"At the Sanibel-Captiva Chamber of Commerce when you were president," Tree said. "You and the lattes changed my life."

"A sad fact for which I will surely be held accountable when

I go off to meet whatever maker is responsible for creating all this shit," Rex said. "I fear the worst once I explain how encouraging your madness may have helped destroy the island's tourist economy, and perhaps the world as we know it."

"Becky is only saying that the world is about to end," Tree pointed out. "She hasn't said I had anything to do with it."

"The Voice, as everyone calls it, simply neglected to mention your name," Rex said. "Press reports of your various misadventures, not to mention your habit of finding dead bodies in the darndest places, have scared people away in droves. The end of the world certainly is not going to help tourism. But that's not the half of it. Wait until it gets out that at the same time, you're renewing your private detective's license. When that happens, they might as well close down the state. We are all doomed."

"Not that I've had much use for a private detective's license lately," Tree said gloomily. "At the end of the world, people are discovering that the last thing they need is a detective."

Gladys Demchuk made her entrance, late as usual, although it should be said that at the offices of the Sanibel Sunset Detective Agency, arriving early or late made little difference since nothing much was happening, anyway.

Supposedly, Gladys had been hired to answer the phone after she arrived in Florida following many years in Los Angeles. With her flaming red hair and whip-thin dancer's body, Gladys still possessed enough appeal to remind anyone who could remember such things that while in L. A. in the 1980s, she had attained a certain notoriety as the adult film star, Blue Streak.

What with age and now amateurs doing for fun what she did for money, Gladys got out of the business and opened her own private L.A. investigation firm, The Bad Actors Detective Agency, made up of former television stars who were in fact, pretty bad actors—and not much better at being real life private detectives.

Fed up with trying to wrangle temperamental actors-turned-detectives and desiring a change of scenery, she had moved to Florida and had landed with Rex and Tree in a back room at the Cattle Dock Bait Company.

Since the phone wasn't ringing very often, Rex had put her to work organizing publicity for his book. It was her job to phone radio and television stations and pitch the former— well, you couldn't really call Rex a *star*. Gladys identified him as a legendary Hollywood veteran who knew all the stars in Tinsel Town, an icon of Chicago broadcasting, the beloved former president of the Sanibel-Captiva Chamber of Commerce, who had written a hard-hitting, tell-it-like-it-is memoir.

When Gladys mentioned that Rex had slept with, among others, Joan Crawford, there were times when the person to whom she was speaking vaguely remembered Joan Crawford. Otherwise, the declaration of Rex's celebrity sex exploits was usually met with either silence or a single questioning word: "Who?"

"They call it the Overview Effect," Gladys pronounced, dropping her handbag onto her desk.

"What's that?" Rex asked.

"It's that first experience of space that turns ordinarily sane people into evangelists preaching the gospel of space. If you ask me, it was a matter of time before someone nuts enough to be out walking in space in the first place, started hearing voices."

"You don't think it's the end of the world?" Rex inquired.

"I'm from Southern California, honey. Out there, it's constantly the end of the world—until it isn't."

"I've got more bad news for you first thing in the morning," Rex said. "Tree is renewing his Florida private detective's license. In anticipation of the trouble to come, people are already fleeing Sanibel."

Gladys turned to Tree with a look of surprise. "I thought you were thinking of retiring."

"I'm continuing to think about it," Tree said.

"Don't listen to him," Rex said. "This would be, by my count, the third time he's announced his retirement."

"I haven't *announced* anything," Tree countered. "I am in the process of *considering* the possibility."

"It's not as though you've been overwhelmed with clients lately," Gladys observed, seating herself at her desk.

The words were hardly out of Gladys's mouth before the telephone on her desk began making vaguely familiar sounds indicating someone was actually calling. The three of them stared at the phone.

"One of us should answer it," Rex suggested. It was at that point that Gladys remembered that was her job and grabbed the receiver. "Sanibel Sunset Detective Agency. Gladys Demchuk speaking. How may I direct your call?"

She listened to the voice on the other end and then said, "Hold on, please. I'll see if he's available." She covered the mouthpiece and said to Tree, "It's for you."

Tree picked up the phone on his desk. "Is this Tree Callister?" asked a male voice.

"It is," affirmed Tree. "How can I help you?"

"Mr. Callister, this is Dwight McPhee calling. You may not remember me, but we met years ago at the Kiwanis spaghetti dinner." The spaghetti dinner was an annual fundraising event that Rex always roped Tree into attending back in the days when he was president of the island's Chamber of Commerce. Not that Tree could remember anyone named Dwight McPhee, unless—

"Mr. McPhee, your daughter isn't by any chance Becky McPhee, the astronaut?"

"That's right. Rebecca, Becky. That's why I'm calling, Mr. Callister. I'd like to speak to you in confidence, if I may."

"Of course," Tree said, thinking that this could be a hoax of some kind before dismissing the notion.

"My daughter is staying with me out here on Captiva. As you can imagine, things have gotten pretty crazy, what with one thing and another."

"I understand," Tree said.

"Most disturbingly, there have been death threats which I am taking seriously. I've put together a security team, made up of the ex-Navy SEALs team Becky worked with back in the day. However, I'd like to add a local component, someone who knows their way around the area. Your name came up, Mr. Callister."

"It did?" Surprise forced the words out of Tree's mouth before he could stop them.

"Would you be interested in helping us out for the next few weeks? I'd certainly make it worth your while."

Fleetingly, Tree thought that even after twelve years kicking around Sanibel and Captiva, he had doubts about how much he knew about the islands. Out loud, he said, "I'd be glad to do anything I can to help you and your daughter, Mr. McPhee."

"Call me, Dwight, please."

"I'm not sure how much I can add to what sounds like a pretty impressive group, Dwight."

"Nonsense. Your reputation precedes you, Mr. Callister."

It does? Tree thought. This time he kept the thought to himself.

"I'm certain you will be an asset to the team," Dwight continued. "We're meeting tomorrow morning at my house on

Captiva. Can you clear your schedule? I'd like you to meet the team, and introduce you to Becky."

Clearing his schedule? That would not be a problem, he thought. "Yes, that's a possibility," Tree said. "Let me check with my assistant but tomorrow should be fine."

"That would be much appreciated, Mr. Callister—"

"Please, call me Tree."

"Much appreciated, Tree. Ten o'clock tomorrow morning. Palm Flower Lane. We're at the end on the left. I'll leave word with security."

"That's fine," Tree said.

"Becky will be giving her first press conference since leaving NASA the following afternoon at the Sanibel Community House. I'd like to have our team in place so that security can be provided."

"I'll be there at ten," Tree said.

"We'll see you then, and thank you—Tree!"

As he hung up, Tree saw Gladys and Rex staring with goggle eyes. "That wasn't Becky McPhee's father, was it?" Gladys asked.

"It was," Tree said.

"He wants you to work for him?"

"As part of the security team he's putting together. Apparently, there have been threats to Becky's life."

"And he wants *you* to protect her?" The disbelief in Rex's voice was undeniable.

"Well, I'm going to be part of a group of ex-navy SEALs, people who served with Becky."

Rex and Gladys traded glances.

"What?" Tree demanded.

"It's just that if you're involved, maybe it really is the end of the world," Rex said.

Gladys managed a weak smile. "Or perhaps you should look at it a little more optimistically," she said.

"How would you suggest I do that?" Rex asked.

"Look at it from the point of view that maybe Tree can ride to the rescue, so to speak," Gladys said. "The Sanibel Sunset Detective saves the world."

That'll be the day, Tree thought.

3

By the time Becky McPhee exited the ISS, there had been over two hundred spacewalks totaling fifteen hundred hours. However, Becky was the only astronaut to claim she heard the Voice in the midst of a spacewalk.

That Voice, according to what Becky reported when she returned to earth, had told her that the world would come to an on the day of the next solar eclipse, Aug. 21. It was now Aug. 12.

Becky's announcement had been made to a world already thrown into turmoil by a global pandemic, as well as climate-related forest fires, hurricanes, blizzards, tsunamis and tornadoes—and not to forget the plagues of cicadas. Millions had viewed Becky's revelation as the logical endgame in a steady, relentless procession of catastrophes. Prayer vigils were being held around the world. Thousands were arriving daily in Florida and many of those headed for Sanibel Island, driven by rumors that Becky was holed up there with her family. These pilgrims had filled the hotels and resorts, the campgrounds and the RV parks. Along Periwinkle Way, hundreds of men, women, and children were on their knees in prayer.

How could the world not take seriously a fortyish astronaut noted for her intelligence and rigorous belief in science, a woman possessed of a feet-on-the-ground cool in the face of adversity. And during her first press conference since arriving back on earth, she had made a compelling case for the Voice in space warning of the world's imminent demise.

When Tree got home to Andy Rosse Lane, his wife, Freddie

Stayner, was watching CNN. "They're interviewing the Russian cosmonaut who was on the space station with Becky," Freddie reported, keeping her eyes on the screen.

The chyron at the bottom of the screen identified a walking, talking blond, square-jawed, blue-eyed poster boy for the greatness of Vladimir Putin's Russia as Yuri Revin. In pretty good English, Yuri was saying, "No, I did not hear anything when Becky and I were together. But I was inside the space station at the time and as you know we were having trouble with the outside cameras, which is why she was out there in the first place."

Anderson Cooper asked him what he thought of the possibility that Becky had heard a voice while she was floating outside the space station. "I do not know about this," Yuri answered after a moment of consideration. "But I do know that when Becky returned, she was quite shaken up."

"Did she tell you she'd heard a voice?" Cooper asked.

"At the time, no," Yuri said. "But as I say, it was obvious something unusual had happened to her."

"If she didn't tell you when it happened, doesn't that raise suspicions as to whether she heard anything at all?"

"I love Becky, I believe Becky," Yuri said. "If Becky says she heard a voice, then I must believe that she heard a voice and we all must take her warning seriously."

"Then do you think the world is coming to an end?" asked Cooper.

That elicited a wry smile from the cosmonaut. "Let me put it this way. Until after the next ten days, I am not making any plans."

"There you go," Tree said as Freddie used the remote control to turn off the television. "Yuri what's-his-face believes Becky's story."

"The Voice… hogwash as far as I'm concerned," said Freddie.

"Hogwash, now there's a word I haven't heard for a long time," Tree said.

"A favorite of my mother's," Freddie said. "In other words, I don't believe it."

"I gather you don't believe that this is the end," Tree observed.

"We're here on Captiva Island, it's a warm night, outside there is a nearly full moon over gently waving palm trees. I'm sipping a glass of chardonnay beside my favorite man, and I have to say life is pretty darned good. You mean to tell me that all this is going to come crashing to an end?"

"I hope you're right," Tree said. "Still, given what we've been through lately, it's hard not to think that anything is possible—which is what much of the rest of the globe, judging from the reaction to Becky's prediction, seems to think as well."

"I'm sorry, call me a cockeyed optimist, but I simply do not believe someone hears a voice and the world vanishes."

"I'll inform Becky of your doubts when I see her tomorrow."

"I feel kind of sorry for her," Freddie said. "You know you have struck a raw nerve in this country when the crazies come out threatening to use their Second Amendment rights to silence you. If they don't want you dead, then they want to see and touch the new Messiah, waiting, lined up along Periwinkle Way. I don't envy her in the least."

"From what Dwight McPhee told me on the phone, it sounds as though a very professional security team is already in place to protect her," Tree said.

"Additionally, there is now that crack defender of damsels and astronauts in distress, Mr. Tree Callister."

"To tell you the truth I'm a little nervous about this," Tree said.

"A little?" Freddie raised an eyebrow.

"All right, a lot. I'm not sure why Dwight thinks he needs me. These guys with Becky are superbly trained ex-Navy SEALs. The best of the best."

"Supposedly," added Freddie.

"I'm only Tree Callister, and I'm not even the Tree Callister I used to be."

"What was the Tree Callister you used to be?" Freddie asked.

"Younger," replied Tree.

"Saner, too. The younger Tree Callister wasn't a private detective and would never have gotten mixed up in something like this."

"You're probably right," Tree said. "But it's too late; I'm old and crazy, prone to doing the unexpected."

"I've come to the conclusion you do these insane things because it's your way of howling against the night, defying death by constantly putting your life at risk."

"That doesn't make any sense," Tree said.

"That's because *you* don't make any sense," Freddie countered.

"That doesn't make any sense, either," Tree said.

"There's something I should probably tell you before you go over there," Freddie said.

"Okay," Tree said.

"Not that it makes any difference to anything, but years ago when I was single in Chicago, I dated Dwight McPhee."

"You're kidding," Tree said. "How long did you date him?"

"I guess we went out for a year or so. He was a hotshot young trader on the Chicago stock exchange and I was a hot young marketing director at the state's largest supermarket chain."

"Was it serious?"

"I'm not sure. It didn't work out so I suppose it couldn't have been too serious."

"But serious enough."

"Well, it went on for a year so whatever that means."

"Why did you break up?"

"From what I can remember, we were both preoccupied with careers and were sort of drifting apart. Then I met the guy who turned out to be my second husband and that was that. We never saw each other again. I hadn't heard much about Dwight for years, until his daughter became an astronaut and started to get attention."

"Why didn't you tell me before now?"

"I probably did when we were first dating and we were trading failed romance stories, but it wouldn't have meant much at the time."

"Was that what it was with Dwight—a failed romance?"

"Yes, I guess it was since it didn't go anywhere."

"Did it end badly?"

Freddie thought about this for a time. "I'm always reminded of *Cocktail*, that otherwise lousy Tom Cruise movie. Tom is breaking up with Elizabeth Shue and he says to her, 'I don't want this to end badly,' and she replies, 'It always ends badly, otherwise it wouldn't end.'"

"The gospel according to Tom Cruise," Tree said dryly.

Freddie gave him a sharp look. "Is this bothering you?"

"I don't know," Tree said. "I don't think it is. He's probably married."

"Dwight's wife died three years ago," Freddie said.

"You know this?"

"I guess I read it somewhere," Freddie said.

"So he's single now," Tree said.

"I imagine he is. Are you sure you're all right with this?"

"It's just kind of weird that you didn't tell me, that's all."

"Tree, I'm married to you. The rest was another lifetime ago. It doesn't make any difference. I love you."

"Even though you think I'm trying to get myself killed in order to convince myself I'm alive."

"Even though," Freddie said with a smile.

"One more question," Tree said. "Did you know Dwight was living here?"

Freddie shrugged. "I'm not sure whether I knew or not. Whatever, it really didn't register."

Still, Tree couldn't help but wonder if he was getting the whole story. How does an old flame move into the neighborhood, and you don't say anything?

How does that happen?

4

NINE DAYS BEFORE THE END OF THE WORLD

Later, Tree mused that if he looked back over the history of his relationships, pre-Freddie, they had all, to paraphrase that masterpiece of cinema, *Cocktail*, ended badly. Thankfully, Freddie had appeared in the nick of time to decisively put an end to his bad-luck-bad-ending streak, his ongoing bafflement as to why his relationships did nothing but, well...*end badly*.

The revelation that Freddie had once dated Dwight McPhee continued to unsettle him despite his protestations to the contrary. Or was jealous a better word than unsettled? Wasn't he too old for jealousy and hadn't he and Freddie been married too long and too successfully for it to now make an appearance? Yes, to both questions. Therefore, *unsettled*, the uneasy feeling that there was something she hadn't told him. The relationship with Dwight had ended, according to Freddy, because, simply, it had ended badly. But when he thought about it, that wasn't really an explanation, was it?

He turned off Captiva Drive onto Palm Flower Lane, a roadway blocked off by Sanibel Island police cruisers. Throngs of mostly elderly people in sun hats and shorts, their faces obscured by dark glasses, straining on either side of the road, anxious, hopeful faces waiting...for what? Some sort of sign from Becky McPhee? When they saw that the guy behind the wheel of the Mercedes wasn't going to provide them with anything, certainly not a sign, the hopeful looks evaporated.

Tree came to a stop and lowered his window as one of the

officers approached, his broad face sweaty from the morning heat. He wore tinted sunglasses and an expression that suggested he was ready in case Tree decided to open fire. Instead of pulling a gun, Tree explained he had an appointment with Dwight McPhee. The cop stepped away to speak into a two-way radio. He nodded and came back to Tree, looking disappointed that there wasn't going to be gunfire and waved him through.

A half mile further on Tree turned into a drive that swept as far as massive iron entrance gates designed to keep the peasants away from the McPhee compound. Tree spoke into the intercom. Occasionally, a peasant had to be allowed inside. This was one of those days. The gates magically opened to admit him.

Tree thought about the number of times he had arrived at the edge of the bubble of the rich on Sanibel and Captiva, walled behind a camouflage of thick foliage, discovering, often thanks to him, that real, dangerous life could slip over the walls to threaten their carefully sheltered world.

Even if you were the uber rich Dwight McPhee and you hired security guards who looked as though they worked out every hour they weren't protecting a client. These were hard-muscled men with what Tree imagined were narrow, suspicious eyes behind those ubiquitous dark glasses, trying to decide as he came through the gate whether he was just another harmless old guy driving a Mercedes or an assassin about to murder everyone in the compound. If they had asked, Tree would have assured them that he occupied a vast, ineffectual middle ground between old guy and assassin—tilting sharply in the direction of old guy.

The dominating structure at the end of a fanlike drive reminded Tree of a brick fortress with a terra-cotta roof. It overlooked a cove that opened onto the glittering jade of San Carlos

Bay. What looked to Tree like two smaller guest houses flanked the main building. Tree left the Mercedes in a parking area near the house, adjacent to a big garage, its doors open to show an impressive array of luxury automobiles. Beyond the garage and through a stand of royal palms, a tennis court shimmered in the morning heat.

As Tree approached the entrance, a young woman appeared and came down the steps lighting a cigarette. In her twenties, cute and voluptuous with dark brown hair falling to her shoulders, she wore a figure-hugging white shorts and a black sleeveless T-shirt. She inspected Tree with a certain insouciance as she blew cigarette smoke in the air.

"If you're making a delivery, you're supposed to go around to the back," she said.

"I'll keep that in mind," Tree said.

"Okay, got it. You're not delivering anything, right?" She blew more smoke.

"I'm here to see Dwight McPhee."

"Daddy's inside with men who look as though they eat nails for breakfast. I'm his daughter, Miranda, incidentally. I'm the one who doesn't hear voices."

"I'm Tree Callister."

"I guess we're not supposed to shake hands any more, are we?"

"It's nice to meet you, Miranda."

"Tree. That's a funny name. You don't look like you eat nails for breakfast or any other time of the day."

"I used to eat nails," Tree said. "But as I got older, I learned they're not healthy."

"That's too bad. You're probably not going to fit in around here," Miranda said.

"The story of my life," Tree said.

"Go right in, Tree. They're all inside trying to figure out how to save my sister's ass—my *older* sister, I should say."

"How about your sister? Is she inside, too?"

She made a performance of glancing around before she said, "Becky is, but I'm not supposed to say anything because people want to kill her because she supposedly heard the Voice. Of course, I grew up with Miss Perfect wanting to kill her every day. But apparently no one's concerned about me."

"Well, I'll make sure I keep an eye on you."

She rewarded him with a sexy pout. "Why Mr. Tree, you old devil, you."

"I'd better get inside," Tree said.

"I think you'd better."

Tree nodded and went up the steps. "Hey," Miranda said, calling after him.

He turned around.

"Good luck," she said.

"Thanks."

"You're going to need it," she added before exhaling more cigarette smoke.

5

An elegant white-haired woman gave Tree a quizzical look as he came into a foyer so glaringly white it made him squint.

"Excuse me," she said in a plummy, British-accented voice. "Did they not tell you? All deliveries are made at the back."

"I'm here to see Dwight McPhee," Tree said. "My name's Tree Callister. I believe he's expecting me."

"*You're* Tree Callister?" The white-haired woman made it sound as though this was simply not a possibility.

"I am," Tree agreed.

"Yes, well then, you are expected," said the white-haired woman looking as though she was trying to dismiss suspicions that Tree did not eat nails for breakfast.

"I'm Karen Lancaster-Simms, Mr. McPhee's personal assistant," the woman continued. "The others are out by the pool having coffee and croissants. Would you care to join them?"

"Are they eating nails?"

The smooth pale porcelain of Karen's face clouded over. "I'm sorry?"

"It's all right," Tree said. "Joining everyone would be swell."

With a final I-don't-quite-believe-this glance, she led Tree out to a pool the size of a small lake. Three big dudes were talking together at one end. They turned at their approach. In the glare of the morning sun, they looked like they could handle anything, including breakfast nails. Searching eyes were hidden behind dark glasses. Muscles rippled beneath short-sleeved Polo shirts. Glock automatics nestled in holsters strapped to their waists. The African American and Caucasian had skulls that looked as though they had been polished first thing that morning. The Asian's full head of rich black hair was the anomaly.

"Gentlemen, I want you to meet Mr. Tree Callister."

"Hey, there," said the Caucasian skull guy. "Are you the hombre who can take our breakfast orders?"

Karen made a slight face. "Tree's here to see Dwight. I'll send out Manuel in a couple of minutes. He can get you anything you'd like to eat."

Caucasian skull guy stuck his hand out. "Sorry about that, pal. I'm Clint Stark. What'd you say your name was again?"

"Tree Callister," Tree said. "But we shouldn't shake hands."

Clint yanked his hand away. "That Covid-19 shit." He turned to the other two. "Our socially correct African American is Chip Holbrook."

"Hey there, Tree," Chip said. "Don't pay any attention to this asshole." He jerked a thumb in Clint's direction. "If he met the president of the United States, he'd ask him for breakfast."

"Most important meal of the day," Clint said. He indicated the third member of the trio. "This lucky son of a bitch checks off the column marked Mysterious Man of the East. Path Yoon who is lucky because he gets to have all his hair."

"Unlucky because I have to work with these pricks," Path said. "Where'd you serve, Tree?"

"I didn't serve," Tree said.

Chip asked, "What are you ex-FBI? CIA? NSA?"

"None of the above," Tree said, starting to feel a little embarrassed at not having worked anywhere with initials.

"Mr. Callister is a private investigator on Sanibel and Captiva." Karen offered this information as though she was a bit embarrassed by it.

Thank goodness for the dark glasses, Tree thought. Otherwise, the three wouldn't have done nearly as good a job masking their reactions. Karen's revelation instead had the effect of producing an uneasy silence.

Finally, Clint ventured, "A private investigator, you say?"

"That's right. Our offices are just off the island."

"On Sanibel?" as though Chip needed confirmation.

"And the surrounding area." Was he sounding a little too defensive?

"I wouldn't have thought there was enough work to keep a private dick in business," Clint said. "Seems pretty quiet around here."

"What are you then?" asked Chip. "Ex-local law enforcement?"

"Actually, I was a newspaperman in Chicago before moving here," Tree said, feeling more inadequate than ever.

Clint adjusted his sunglasses to get a better look at Tree, as though he couldn't trust his lying eyes. "Newspaperman, huh? Fake news, right?"

"Just for fun, we sometimes used actual facts," Tree said.

"I believe the idea is that Mr. Callister will act as our local security liaison," Karen put in helpfully. Then she moved back as though suddenly it was not a good idea to be too close to Tree. "Excuse me while I let Dwight know you're here," she said to him. "As I understand it, he wants to go over a few things with you."

As soon as Karen entered the house, Clint removed his sunglasses so that Tree had a good view of burning, coal-black eyes—a killer's eyes, he couldn't help thinking. "Listen to me bro'." Clint didn't so much speak as whisper between gritted teeth. "These dudes and me, we were SEALs together with Becky, okay? Served in the Afghanistan together, so we're brothers and sisters, a close-knit group. As close as it gets."

"I understand," Tree said, trying keep the nervousness out of his voice.

"Now she's in trouble, and that's enough for the three of us to come running. We don't give a rat's ass if she saw Jesus dancing on the roof of the space station, she needs our help and that's the end of it. We're professionals, cast in the heat of combat and therefore, believe me, we know what the hell we're doing."

"I'm sure you do," Tree said.

"We know how to protect her, we can and will do that," Clint continued, "but Tree, where do you fit into this operation? Right now, I don't see it. I mean, no offence, but look at you. You're a civilian, and that means one thing. You know what that is?"

"Why don't you tell me, Clint?"

"It means you're only going to get in the way. You get in the way and someone turns up dead, and I'm telling you that's not going to happen on my watch."

He stepped even closer, his eyes burning with a zealot's brightness. "You got that, old man?"

"That's enough, Clint." The four turned in unison to see Karen coming toward them guiding a man leaning hard on a cane.

"Gentlemen," she said, "I think most of you have already met Mr. Dwight McPhee."

"Yes," Dwight said. "But I haven't met Mr. Callister." He hobbled forward to Tree. "I guess I shouldn't shake your hand, Tree. But it's good to finally meet you. I hope Clint hasn't managed to scare you too much."

"He just scared me a little bit," Tree said, lying through his teeth.

"Well, don't let him scare you at all." Dwight turned to the others. "I've personally requested Tree's presence here. I want the three of you to respect that. Understood?"

He waited until the three SEALs nodded assent before smiling at Tree. The smile dropped years off Dwight McPhee and if you weren't already impressed with his six-foot-three height, the craggy, square-jawed authority in his tanned face, then the smile sealed the deal. You'd follow Dwight just about anywhere and give him money along the way which, from the look of things, that's exactly what a lot of people over the years had done.

Tree couldn't help but think, *damn*, this was the sort of guy Freddie should have married. Instead, she had ended up with him, a guy whose smile had failed to induce anyone to follow him anywhere let alone give him any money.

And then it struck Tree that if Freddie should have married Dwight, then Dwight might well be thinking all these years later that he should have married Freddie. And now here he was on Sanibel Island, not far away from the woman he regretted not marrying. How would you get close to that woman again after all this time?

Well, for starters, you might hire her husband.

6

They adjourned to a table beneath an awning at the far end of the pool. As staff in white coats served coffee and croissants, the three ex-SEALs unhappily inspected Tree out of what he imagined were the corners of the eyes hidden behind those dark glasses.

Dwight lowered himself into a chair using the cane for support. He appeared to be in pain until he was properly seated. Once he was, he thrust his chin in Tree's direction. "Suffered a stroke a year ago," he explained. "A couple of years after my wife died. Damnedest thing."

"Sorry to hear that," Tree said.

"What with my wife gone, and the stroke, various business difficulties, it's all worked to knock me off my stride a bit, but I'm coming back, stronger than ever—just takes time; time and determination. Believe me, I've got both."

"Good for you," Tree said, thinking that at least he had yet to suffer a stroke. Hopefully, Freddie would see that as a plus. A crippled billionaire versus a broken-down former newspaper reporter trying to be a private detective on an island where nothing ever happened. No competition as far as Tree was concerned. The guy trying to be a private detective would win hands down.

Wouldn't he?

Dwight was addressing the others. "As I told you before, I've asked Tree to become part of our team for the next while. I imagine Karen has already explained to you that Tree is here as our man on Sanibel and Captiva. He's not going to be gunning down anyone who comes for Becky. That's what you gentlemen are here for and I trust you'll do the job that needs to be done."

"Roger that," said Clint in the sort of commanding voice that suggested he was ready to start shooting right now.

"Tree will be our go-to if any of you guys turn left on Periwinkle when you should turn right."

"Where's Periwinkle?" Chip asked.

"I rest my case," Dwight said with a laugh.

The follow-up laughter was brittle and artificial. The boss laughed; therefore, the employees laughed.

"All right, let's get down to business," Dwight continued. "Clint, how'd you like to bring Tree up to speed on what's been done thus far? It'll also serve as a refresher for me and the others."

"Roger that, Mr. McPhee," Clint said. He shot a glance at Tree, and then leaned forward taking in the others.

"Okay, we've completed a risk assessment to ascertain the level of danger for Becky. No surprise that what with the attention she has recently received, the crowds of people on the island and in the surrounding area, many of whom appear, to put it as diplomatically as possible, to be experiencing emotional problems, coupled with the controversial nature of her statements that have received huge amounts of attention—put all that together and you have to conclude that Becky is at very high risk."

Clint paused to allow everyone at the table to digest this. No one argued with him.

He continued: "All the warning signs we look for as SEALs are present in this environment: uncertainty, turbulence and volatility. In order to get control of the situation in the next while and ensure that Becky is protected, agility is the name of the game."

Tree wasn't sure what that meant, but everyone else nodded in solemn agreement. "A small highly trained core group"—Clint noticeably did not look at Tree when he said this—"that can anticipate trouble and move at a moment's—"

Clint stopped talking as a small, slim woman, barefoot, wearing a T-shirt and shorts slipped into view. Tree realized with a start that Becky McPhee was joining them. Pale blond hair was cropped short, tangled around a clear round face without makeup, blue eyes so opaque they were almost otherworldly. Becky McPhee might have come in peace from another planet, Tree thought. You could believe that easily enough. Harder to imagine the combat-hardened former Navy SEAL.

"Sorry, I'm late," she said in a voice not much above a whisper. She bent to give her father a quick hug before she slipped into the empty chair beside Tree.

"Would you like some coffee, honey?" Dwight asked.

"No, I'm fine." The opaque blue eyes darted toward Tree.

"Becky, you haven't met the newest member of the team, Tree Callister," Dwight said.

The eyes stopped darting and engaged Tree full on, making him feel curiously uneasy. Dwight continued, "Tree is a private investigator in the area and as we discussed, he is joining us this morning."

"It's a pleasure to meet you," Tree said to her.

Becky reacted by nodding disinterestedly, hunched in her seat, head down, as though preparing for a blow.

"Glad you could join us Becky," Clint said casting her a worried glance.

"Clint," she said, giving out a smile that was gone as quickly as it arrived.

Clint nodded and then shifted so that he was once again addressing the table. "Okay, our number one priority for the moment is tomorrow's press conference at the Sanibel Community House. As Mr. McPhee is aware, we are working with a private security firm out of Miami. I know these people and they're damned good. In addition to the operatives they've got here at the compound, they're providing an additional six people to help us secure the press conference."

"This is crazy." Becky spoke in such a low voice that Clint wasn't sure he had heard her.

"I'm sorry?" Clint leaned toward her.

In a slightly raised voice, Becky said, "I said, this is crazy. It's a press conference. It's no big deal."

Dwight stiffened and then said, "We've talked about this, Becky. There are all sorts of crazies around and more arriving every day. Clint believes we must take these threats and the possibility of trouble seriously. I agree with him. Let's get through this thing tomorrow, do as we're being advised, and then reassess the situation."

"Whatever," Becky mumbled. She seemed to sink further into the chair.

Dwight turned his attention to Tree. "I'd like you to accompany Chip over to the Community House, Tree. You know the place. Have a look around, make sure everything's all right."

"Sure," Tree said.

"You okay with that, Chip?" Dwight asked.

Chip nodded without showing any sign of enthusiasm at the prospect of partnering with Tree.

A portly young man with a pale, unshaven face and a shock of blond hair, his white belly overhanging orange swimming trunks, sauntered past without acknowledging anyone at the table. He reached the pool, balanced on the edge and performed an impressive dive, slicing smoothly into the water and then executing a swift breaststroke.

The portly swimmer reached the end and lifted himself out of the pool. With water dripping off him, he ambled along the pool deck to the table. "How's everyone this morning?" he asked, his tone suggesting he could care less. "My name's Theodore McPhee. Everyone calls me Tad. My father, he's not gonna introduce me because he's afraid of what I might say to you all." His gaze fell on Tree. "This guy, for example, like, who are you?"

"I'm Tree Callister," said Tree.

"*You*—you're gonna be protecting my sister? Look at you." Ambivalence had become a sneer. "I mean what is this? Some kind of joke? What are you gonna do, Elm Tree? Beat off the bad guys with your cane?"

"That's enough, Tad. We're in the midst of a meeting." Dwight spoke quietly, but there was a strained tone.

"Sure, a meeting. Go for it. But let me tell you all something that may not be on your agenda this morning. It's the fact that my sister needs protection all right—but you know who she needs protection from? She needs protection from herself."

"Go screw yourself, Tad," Becky didn't look up at her brother as she spoke.

"Funny, how it turns out, isn't it? For years everyone thought I was the nut case in this family." He looked at Becky. "And now look what's happened. It turns out you're loonier than all the rest of us put together—and believe me there's no shortage of loons in this—"

"Tad!" The raised, angry voice of Dwight McPhee cut off his son. He leaned hard on the cane to struggle to his feet. "Get the hell out of here—now!"

Tad forced a smile. "Hey, hey, take it easy, Daddy dear. I am moving on. I guess the advice I'm offering isn't what anyone wants to hear." He gave a nod to the table. "Nice meeting you all. Try not to shoot any tourists. Meantime, I think I'll go off, mix myself a nice Bloody Mary and wait for the end of the world. It's coming, right Becky?"

"Go to hell, Tad," Becky murmured.

"Apparently that's where we're all headed," Tad said.

As he wandered off, Dwight slumped back into his chair, face red, working to catch his breath. "Sorry about that, gentlemen. We're all under a lot of strain these days. Some of us respond better than others."

Becky, head lowered, mumbled something Tree didn't catch.

"What did you say?" demanded her father.

Becky raised her head. "I said Tad's an asshole."

"He's your brother," snapped Dwight.

"He's still an asshole."

Chip turned to Tree. "What do you say we get ourselves over to this Community House?"

"Good idea," chimed in Clint.

Becky immediately jumped up and stormed away.

Exasperated, Dwight turned to Tree. "As you can see, we're all a little tense."

"I understand," Tree said.

"Before you head over, I'd like to have a word with you, Tree—inside."

"Sure," Tree said, wondering what Dwight wanted to talk about.

Wondering what he had gotten himself into.

7

"Can I get you anything, Tree?" Dwight McPhee asked once they had settled on the leather couches set near a mahogany desk you could land a plane on, flanked by computer screens like monoliths from *2001: A Space Odyssey*. "How about a drink?" he added as an afterthought.

"No, I'm fine thanks," Tree said, feeling distinctly uncomfortable sitting alone with Dwight in what his host would probably describe as a study. Floor-to-ceiling windows allowed in the sunlight and a view of San Carlos Bay. You knew you were rich on Sanibel Island if you had a view of San Carlos Bay. Tree had dealt with enough rich people over the years so that he could testify to that.

"Too early in the day or you don't drink?" Dwight asked.

"It's early in the day and I don't drink anymore," Tree answered.

"I wish I could say the same. These days it's never too early it seems."

"Is that so?"

"With this damned stroke and the fallout from that." Dwight raised his cane as though to illustrate the fallout. "And now with this current...situation." He smiled wanly. "It's enough to drive a man to drink."

As if on cue the white-coated staffer made his appearance, a young man, who, with his fine jaw and blazing blue eyes, could be Dwight McPhee's son. "Can I get you anything, Mr. McPhee?"

"A light gin and tonic, if you will, Jimmy." He pointed to Tree. "Sure I can't interest you in something?"

Tree shook his head. "The gin and tonic, Jimmy," Dwight said. "That's fine."

Jimmy nodded and disappeared. Dwight shifted on the sofa and it struck Tree that he might be just as uncomfortable as he was.

"I wanted to talk to you alone for a few minutes," Dwight said. "You know, so that we could get to know each other a little better. Between now and tomorrow afternoon, there may not be a lot of time."

"Are you really expecting trouble?" Tree asked.

Dwight made a non-committal gesture with his hand. "Frankly, I don't know what to expect. Becky wanted those Navy SEAL fellows with her. Then they got here and as you heard out at the pool, now she gives every indication she doesn't want them. So I don't know. I thought at my age I'd gotten to be a pretty smart fellow, but as this goes on, I'm beginning to realize how little I know about anything."

"How about the world ending? What do you think about that?"

Dwight returned the question with a smile. "What do you think, Tree?"

"For what it's worth, my wife doesn't think it's going to end and over the years I've learned that she is usually more right than wrong."

"Ah, yes, your wife. Fredryka. Freddie."

Tree didn't like the fact that Dwight's eyes appeared to brighten as he spoke Freddie's name.

"How is she doing?"

"She's fine," Tree said. "Enjoying her retirement."

"Freddie retired." Dwight shook his head. "Hard to imagine. Did she tell you that we used to date in Chicago?"

"She mentioned it," Tree said.

"Mentioned it?" Dwight couldn't hide a flash of disappointment.

"From what I understand, it was a long time ago," Tree said.

Dwight's smile was surprisingly winsome. "Funny, when I think about it, it seems like yesterday."

Tree swallowed the urge to say, Well, it wasn't.

Dwight's pale-blue eyes fell on Tree. "But instead, she married you." Delivered like an accusation.

"Yes, in a moment of weakness I'm sure," Tree said. "But ever since, she's insisted on staying married to me."

Dwight didn't respond, keeping his eyes on Tree. The silence in the room began to make them both uncomfortable.

"When I knew Freddie, I was only rich," he said at last. "All these years later, I'm not just rich, I'm stupid rich. Insanely rich. The sort of rich that doesn't buy you much other than a lot of problems." He nodded out the window. "You're seeing some of that today."

"I'm not sure what I'm supposed to say to that," Tree said.

"Nothing to say." Dwight cleared his throat. "It's good to have you aboard, Tree. And you know what? It would be great to see Freddie again." He added a smile to the notion. "That is if you don't mind."

"Not at all," Tree said. "I'm sure Freddie would like to see you, too."

"Let's see what we can arrange. Dinner, maybe. How's that?"

"Sounds good," Tree said, although he didn't think it sounded very good at all.

"I won't hold you up any longer," Dwight said. "I'm sure Chip must be waiting."

Tree nodded and stood. "Good to have you aboard," Dwight repeated.

Tree wondered.

As he left, Jimmy entered through another door with the gin and tonic.

Miranda McPhee waited in the corridor. "I was listening at the door," she announced as Tree approached.

"Did you hear anything interesting?" Tree asked.

"The husband of the old flame," Miranda said with a smirk. "I thought I might have to come to your rescue if Daddy started beating you with his cane."

"Why would he do that?"

"You got what he wanted, and Daddy doesn't like that."

"No?"

"I don't know whether he mentioned it or not, but Daddy usually gets what he wants—no matter how long it takes."

"I'll keep that in mind," Tree said.

"Good idea," Miranda said. Her smile as Tree passed would best be described as lascivious.

Chip was leaning against the side of a Range Rover as Tree came out of the house. "I was beginning to wonder what happened to you," Chip said, unfolding his arms and moving away from the vehicle. He spotted Miranda McPhee as she came out behind Tree.

"Wait in the Land Rover," Chip said. "I'll be right back."

Miranda's face softened as Chip approached her—a lot happier than she had looked confronting Tree. She took Chip's hand. He pulled it away. She looked disappointed, and said something that made Chip gesture helplessly and then turn back to the Land Rover. Meanwhile, Miranda flounced away into the house, slamming the door behind her.

"Everything all right?" Tree inquired as Chip slid into the passenger seat.

"Why shouldn't it be?" snapped Chip. "Every meal's a banquet. Every paycheck is a fortune. Every day's a goddamn paradise. Let's get out of here."

8

Television trucks with big white satellite dishes were crowded at the side of the one-story frame Sanibel Community House, an island landmark since 1927. More broadcast trucks jammed the field on the other side of Periwinkle Way.

At noontime, impatient reporters and photographers were being held back by metal barriers. A large crowd, Tree thought, considering that the press conference wasn't until the following afternoon.

"Can you believe this shit?" Chip said, maneuvering past a Sanibel police officer directing traffic so he could turn into the parking area.

"Goddamn circus," Chip continued, steering the Range Rover around the broadcast trucks to reach the back of the building. "The whole damn thing's a circus." He glanced at Tree. "Tell me what you thought of that little show this morning."

"I'm not sure what to think," Tree said honestly

"Hey, I love Becky. She's the real deal. But the rest of the family? Goddamn bunch of whack-nuts."

"Then you believe she heard a voice when she was walking in space?"

A hovering security guard recognized Chip and with a wave guided him into an empty parking space. Chip kept talking as he backed in the Range Rover.

"Who knows? I mean when I served with Becky, man, she was rock steady. I didn't know what to think when I first met her. A woman joining our unit in Afghanistan? Come on.

What's that all about? But man, she was a real road warrior, let me tell you. No voices in the Hindu Kush mountains, that's for certain, just a lot of sons of bitches who want to kill you. And she was as tough as they come; that woman had our backs over there, and now we've got hers. Whether there's a Voice, as Clint said, doesn't mean shit. She's in trouble, we're gonna help her out, no questions, end of story."

Chip had brought the SUV to a stop and turned off the engine. He looked over at Tree. "You know what's so funny? When we were in Afghanistan, she told me she'd enlisted so she could get away from her crazy family. Now here she is back in Florida, trapped with her crazy family. Wild, eh?"

He didn't give Tree a chance to answer before he went on. "Tell you one thing, though. If it were me and I knew the shit that would hit the fan back on earth, I would have kept my big mouth shut about any voice I happened to pick up in space."

He turned off the engine and bounded out of the Range Rover, heading for a rear entrance. Tree trotted along behind and together they entered a kitchen and then into a good-sized meeting hall. A podium had been set up at one end. A couple of workmen were unloading ranks of chairs and setting them in rows before the podium.

Chip had stopped and turned around to Tree. "Well? You see any imminent threats, given your vast knowledge of our location?"

"Not at the moment," Tree said. "What about you?"

"I'm gonna check out the bathrooms," Chip said.

"Just out the door and off to the right of the reception area," Tree said.

"There you go, Tree, you're already making yourself useful."

"Anything I can do to help," Tree said.

Chip disappeared out the door, leaving Tree to watch the workmen finishing lining up the chairs.

As he stood there wondering what to do with himself, Tree heard the door in the kitchen bang open. A moment later, a familiar figure stalked into view.

Well, not all that familiar.

The Tommy Dobbs Tree had first met over a decade before was rail thin with a pale, acned face that never saw sunlight. That Tommy Dobbs never separated his whites from his dark colors when he did a laundry and therefore his white shirts were a sickly gray and frayed at the collars.

This Tommy Dobbs, the one coming toward him now with a big grin on a healthy face clear of acne, this Tommy Dobbs had filled out considerably. The hair that had formerly been an unkempt mess was now a tribute to an anonymous-but-expensive stylist. Tommy Bahama linen had replaced the badly washed gray shirts of the past. Tommy Dobbs was no longer Tommy Dobbs, the desperate local reporter badgering Tree for a story. Now he was Thomas Dobbs, the accomplished Chicago reporter—but still badgering Tree for a story.

"I thought I saw you come in here, Mr. Callister," Tommy said.

"You're not supposed to be in here, Tommy," Tree said, a sentence he had repeated to Tommy many times over the years—to little effect.

"You may have forgotten since the last time we met, but I'm now known as Thomas," Tommy said.

"All right, Thomas. Get out of here, Thomas."

"The question I have for you, Mr. Callister, is what are *you* doing here?"

"I'm part of Becky McPhee's security detail, which is why I shouldn't be seen talking to a reporter—which I imagine is why you're here."

"Are you kidding?" said Tommy excitedly. "This is the story of the century. Who knows, maybe the last story of *any* century. And look at you, Mr. Callister," added Tommy, sounding very pleased. "Here you are on the inside of the story."

There was a predatory gleam in Tommy's eyes that Tree had become all-too acquainted with.

"Don't even think about it, Tommy—Thomas," Tree admonished. "I can't help you."

"I know, I know, you always say that."

"This time I mean it," Tree said, trying to sound as though he really did mean it.

"How is she? How is Becky doing?"

"Tommy..."

"Okay, okay. I understand." Tommy fished a card out of his pocket. "Here's my cellphone number. Call me, okay? Strictly between the two of us. Anonymous source, all that stuff."

"Tommy, I'm not going to help you."

"Maybe we can help each other," Tommy went on.

"I don't need any help, Tommy. I need you to get out of here."

"Listen to me for a moment. You know who Dwight McPhee is, right?"

"Do I, Tommy? It sounds as though you're going to tell me I don't."

"You probably don't know this." Tommy dropped his voice to the conspiratorial level that he had used in the past when imparting information to Tree. "Dwight runs the McPhee Group, a bigtime hedge fund, right? That's how he's made his millions. Well, here's the thing. Last year, the Chicago office of the FBI quietly opened an investigation into alleged insider trading, McPhee paying for information that supposedly netted his fund fifty million dollars in profits. From what I hear, the FBI was about to charge him and ten others, when Becky shot into space and became America's sweetheart."

Tree glanced around nervously, expecting Chip to return at any moment.

"Becky arrives back on earth. The FBI still plans to move against Dwight," Tommy went on. "But before they can make an arrest, Becky announces that she's heard the Voice telling her the world is going to end with a solar eclipse. Everyone goes crazy at the news and so the FBI stands down."

"What are you saying, Tommy?"

"Not saying anything, Mr. Callister. But I am here to get the facts and let those facts take me to the story."

"That this is all a scam cooked up in order to keep Becky's father out of jail?"

"You said it, Mr. Callister. Not me." Tommy leaned closer and dropped his voice to a whisper. "This is the angle I'm pursuing down here: Becky's family thinks she's nuts and that all this voice stuff is designed to deflect attention away from her father. Have you heard anything about that?"

"Tommy, I just got involved in this," Tree said. "I don't know anything."

"You think it's a scam, Mr. Callister?"

"I think you'd better get the hell out of here before I'm seen talking to you, which is not going to help either one of us."

"Then I can count on you, Mr. Callister?"

"Right now, I need you out of here."

Tommy started off, his face alive with excitement. "You've got my number, call me, okay?" He ginned mischievously. "I knew that I'd run into you, and I knew that somehow you'd be involved in this—"

"Tommy, get out," Tree said.

"Call me." Tommy disappeared into the kitchen as Chip

came back into the room, his face set into an expression of suspicion.

"Who was that?" he demanded.

"Some guy who wandered in here," Tree said. "I told him to get out."

"Yeah?" Chip responded by looking even more suspicious. "You up to something, Tree? Something I should know about?"

"I don't know, Chip. What do you think I'm up to?"

"Talking to that guy. What was that all about?"

"I told you. He came in here. I told him to get out."

The sound of Chip's cellphone broke the tension.

"Yeah, it's all clear here," he announced to whoever was on the line. "Tree?" He glanced quickly in Tree's direction. "Yeah, he tells me he's been keeping the area clear, and, hey, the dude helped me find the bathrooms. Indispensable, I'd say." Chip gave Tree a thumbs up. "You want to talk to him?" he asked. "Okay, hold on."

Chip jabbed his cellphone at Tree. "Boss man for you."

"For me?"

"Yeah. Can you believe that?"

Tree took the phone. "Hey, Tree," Clint said. "How's everything there?"

"Quiet," Tree answered.

"The way we like it," Clint said. "Listen to me. Turns out we're short a man tonight. You up for a taking on a watch at the compound?"

Tree wasn't sure what that meant but he didn't feel as though he had a lot of choice. "Sure, I can do that," he said.

"Good enough," Clint said. "As soon as you're finished at the Community House, get back here. Got it?"

"Yeah, got it," Tree said

The line went dead.

Chip took his cellphone back. "Well," he said with a smirk, "looks like Becky couldn't be safer now that Commander Tree is on duty."

Chip started away and then seemed to have second thoughts. He turned to face Tree up close, his eyes hard and unblinking. "I don't like what happened just now with that dude, you understand that?"

"I don't know what you're talking about," Tree said.

"I got a sense of you, Tree. Maybe you're not the old fart civilian everyone thinks you are. Maybe you're something else. I got my eye on you. Don't forget that."

No, Tree thought as he followed Chip out. He was not going to forget.

9

I'm not sure I need to be wearing this," Tree said as Clint and Chip unceremoniously strapped him into a Kevlar vest.

"It's for when someone shoots you," Clint said.

"Is someone going to shoot me?"

"Well, that's the thing about security, isn't it, Tree?" said Chip dryly. "You just never know."

"I would have thought a seasoned private investigator like yourself would know that," Clint added.

"Yeah, right," Tree said.

When they were finished, they stepped back to inspect their handiwork.

"Something is lacking," Chip said twisting his head at an angle as though to get a better view.

"Plenty is lacking," added Clint. He produced a Glock pistol and handed it to Tree butt first. Tree balanced it uneasily in the palm of his hand.

"It's a gun," said Chip.

"I realize that," Tree said.

"You use it to shoot people," Chip said,

"Any people? Or do you have specific people in mind?"

That got smiles from Clint and Chip. "It's up to you," Clint said. "My rule of thumb is shoot at the people who are shooting at you."

"Good advice," Tree said.

"Last thing," Clint said, handing Tree a palm-sized radio. "Tech1 GRMS, hand-held. Highly reliable. Good for up to thirty-five miles, but you won't need that range tonight. Any trouble, you call it in, pronto. A mosquito looks out of place, call it in. Got that?"

"I think so," Tree said.

"Okay, soldier," Clint said. "You're on duty until midnight at which time you'll be relieved. I need you to keep an eye on the front of the house and the drive. We've got people down by the gate, but you might check on them every so often. You hungry?"

"It's all right. I'll get something once I'm finished here."

"If you change your mind, let me know. Also, Path Yoon is just around the corner watching the rear. He's got an AK-47 in case extra firepower is required."

"Let's hope we don't," Tree said.

"Yeah, well, I'm a bit of an action junkie, Tree." There was a steely glint in Clint's eye as he spoke. "Bring on the shit, I say. That's what we're here for, taking care of the shit."

"Roger that," Tree said without enthusiasm.

———

"Where are you?" Freddie demanded an hour later when Tree called her.

"I'm on guard duty," Tree said.

"What? Where?"

"I'm part of the security detail guarding Becky McPhee."

"You are?" The amazement in Freddie's voice was undeniable.

"Don't sound so surprised. I have a Kevlar vest, a gun, and I've even got a two-way radio."

"They gave you a...*gun?*"

"Which I'm only supposed to use if someone is shooting at me."

"Good advice," Freddie said. "But who do they expect to shoot at you?"

"In all seriousness, there are a lot of crazy people around these days, although I do wonder if some of those crazies aren't right here with Becky."

"Does that include Becky?"

"I'm beginning to wonder," Tree said. "Incidentally, her father was asking about you."

"Dwight?"

"He thinks we should all get together after all this settles down."

"What did you say to that?"

"I said, sure, why not?"

"Did you, really?"

"He's had a stroke, you know."

"No," Freddie said. "I hadn't heard. How would I know that?"

"He has to use a cane. He's old, decrepit."

"Tree Callister, I do believe you're jealous."

"Not at all," replied Tree mildly. "I'm simply reporting the facts, as I always do."

As Tree spoke, he saw someone move in the shadows of the house. Path Yoon came into view, cradling his AK-47.

"I'd better go," Tree said to Freddie

"Please, please be careful."

"I'm always careful."

"No, you're not—and quit being so jealous."

Tree closed his phone as Path approached. "You're not supposed to be on your phone," he said. His face was stern.

"Just letting my wife know where I am," Tree said.

"You tell her you are in Crazyland?"

"Is that where I am?"

That got something approaching a smile from Path. "What do you think?"

"Well, it's a weird situation, that's for sure."

"The other two, Clint and Chip, they think the sun shines out Becky's ass. Me, I'm not so sure."

"But here you are, protecting her," Tree said.

"Paying job," Path said. "They want a man with a gun, I'm a man with the gun." He raised the AK-47 as though to demonstrate the truth of that statement.

"You expecting trouble?"

"I always expect trouble—you should expect it too. Why they've got us out here." He nodded at Tree. "And stay off your phone."

He moved back into the darkness.

Not knowing quite what to do with himself—expect trouble, Path had advised—he wandered down the drive, trying to get himself into a mindset where he could be on the lookout for trouble. Instead of trouble though, he got the cicadas and the night silence. There was a half-full moon crossed by trailing clouds.

The heat was like a blanket around him. He began to perspire under his Kevlar vest and he needed to scratch in areas he couldn't reach because of the vest. Guard duty was beginning to be not only uncomfortable but also boring.

He wandered a bit further down the drive checking along the way that no homicidal maniacs lurked in the foliage or behind the palm trees. Behind him, the main house loomed against the night, pale light visible in a few of the windows but otherwise in darkness. The McPhees apparently had turned in early.

Except not everyone had turned in.

Tree wasn't sure where he came from, but suddenly a figure

appeared and to his disbelieving eyes, seemed to be dancing in the moonlight. Was this the killer he was protecting Becky from? It was hard to tell. Was he supposed to pull out his gun in this instance? A split-second decision was required, was it not? Except he could not make any decision at all.

As he drew closer, Tree could see that the man was naked and waving something around in his hand.

It was Tad McPhee and he was waving a gun.

10

As Tree got closer, Tad swirled around and stopped dancing. The gun looked like it was a .45 automatic pistol, held loosely as he swayed in the moonlight, his face sweaty, eyes dull and puzzled, narrowing to get a better look at Tree.

"Target practice," he mumbled, raising the gun.

"What are you shooting at?" Tree asked.

"I'm considering my head," Tad replied.

"I wouldn't do that."

"No? Why not? I'm looking for targets I can hit easily. My head is easy."

"Why don't you give me the gun so I can see what I can hit?"

Tad's eyes grew wary. "I give you my gun…how am I gonna shoot at my head…?"

"I don't think you want to do that, Tad."

"Target practice," he repeated, staring down at the gun in his hand, as though trying to decide what to do with it. "You hit the target, everything goes away…"

"Not a good idea." Tree's mind was whirling, trying to remember what you said that could bring down a suicidal drunk with a gun. He couldn't remember a thing.

Tad shook his head and his expression became one of pity. "You just don't know, do you?"

"Know what?"

"You don't know what kind of shit you're in. You think you're protecting her from the barbarians at the gates, you poor miserable fool, you are…*among* the barbarians—they are in here…"

Tad wheeled away, raising the .45, more or less pointing it at his head and for one heart-stopping moment, Tree was certain he was going to pull the trigger. Split second decision time—Tree lunged at Tad, managing to knock the gun away, and at the same time sending Tad spilling to the pavement.

The gun lay a few feet away. Tree bent down to scoop it up. Tad, lying on his back, began to laugh. "You stupid bastard," he said in a slurred voice, "you really think I was going to do it? You really thought I was gonna blow my head off...I frigging do this all the time...this place it's made me crazy, don't you see...don't you goddamn see...?"

He began sobbing and as he lay on the ground, he rolled onto his side. Tree tossed the gun into nearby bushes and then knelt to Tad. "Come on," he said, "let's get you inside. How's that?"

"Leave me alone," Tad said, tears streaming down his face. "I want to be left alone."

But he didn't resist as Tree helped him get to his feet. As he attempted to move Tad up the steps, the front door opened and Becky came out, dressed in a T-shirt and shorts. "Jesus," she said when she saw the two of them.

"Becky, you bitch," Tad said when he saw her.

"Here," she said coming down the steps to Tree. "Let me give you a hand."

"He had a gun," Tree said as Becky took Tad's other arm.

"Bastard thought I was going to shoot myself...crazy. Why would I ever do that? Living in paradise with my loony bitch sister, why would I ever do that... I wouldn't want to mess up your carefully laid plans, sister dear..."

"That's enough, Tad," Becky said.

"What?" he mumbled. "You afraid I'm going to tell this old fart what you're up to? Is that what's got you worried?"

"Let's get him inside," Becky said to Tree.

"No, you don't have to worry about good old Tad," he muttered as Tree propped him up. "Want my gun…give me my gun."

He went limp against Tree. With Becky's help, he managed to get Tad up the steps and through the open entrance door. Together, they dragged him across the foyer and into a vast sitting room where they deposited him on a sofa. Tad tried to sit up, groaned and then fell back. Soon, he began to snore.

"He'll be all right," Becky said, standing over him.

"Is he on something?" Tree asked.

"Better to ask what isn't he on. Booze, pills, maybe a line or two of cocaine. Take your pick. This isn't the first time this has happened, probably won't be the last. He's screwed up." She gave a rueful smile. "We're all screwed up. I suppose. Welcome to the McPhee family of crazies."

"Does that include you?" Tree asked.

"Hey, I'm the one who heard the Voice, remember?"

"Incidentally, the gun Tad had, it's outside in some bushes," Tree said.

"Don't worry about it, I'll find it," Becky said.

"What's all this?" Clint came through the foyer into the sitting room. He was bare chested and he had a gun in his hand. "What the hell?" Clint said.

"Where were you?" Becky demanded.

"In bed, where do you think?"

"With my sister?"

Clint looked at Tad. "What's with him?"

"While you were banging my sister, thank goodness for Mr. Callister here. He was able to take care of the situation."

"Yeah? What situation is that?" Clint eyed Tree angrily.

"He did what you should have done," Becky said.

"Tad?"

"Yeah, Tad," Becky confirmed.

"I'm not his goddamn babysitter," Clint said defensively.

"Go back to bed with Miranda, Clint," Becky said. "Everything's under control—once again." She sounded tired.

"It's all right," Clint said, still visibly tense. "It's just about time to relieve Tree, anyway." He nodded at Tree. "Come on, I'll see you out."

"One of Tad's guns is in the bushes outside," Becky said.

"I'll find it," Clint said. To Tree: "Come along, let's get you out of here."

Tree started to follow Clint toward the door. Becky called after him. "Mr. Callister…"

Tree turned to her. "Thanks," she said.

As they came down the steps, Clint produced a cigarette and lit it. He paused at the bottom of the steps to exhale smoke into the air. "Well, there you go, Tree," he said. "Trial by fire. Your introduction to the McPhee family."

"Is Tad always like this?"

"Not always, just every other day or so." Clint blew more smoke in the air. "When I first got the call for this, I thought we'd be protecting Becky from outside enemies. Now I'm beginning to wonder if the enemies are outside…"

"That's what Tad said—the barbarians are in here."

"Tad's nuts, but he's not wrong."

"What was all that in there about Becky's sister?"

Clint gave Tree a look that was part assessment and part suspicion. He took a final drag on the cigarette and then dropped it to the ground and used his foot to stomp it out. "Get some sleep," he said. "I'll see you tomorrow. Should be interesting."

11

Freddie was waiting up for Tree when he got back to Andy Rosse Lane. They sat at the kitchen table while he devoured the leftover chicken and a salad and told her about the night's events.

You're lucky her brother didn't shoot you," observed Freddie.

"I'm not sure if he'd really shoot himself or anyone else, or if he's just looking for attention."

"But you told me he was pretty high."

"Very high from what I could tell," Tree said.

"Then anything could have happened—including you getting shot."

"It's a pretty bizarre situation over there," Tree said. "Everyone stuck together, the true believers outside certain the world is about to end, this family on the inside, with a suicidal brother, one sister who is back from space having heard the Voice, and another sister who is keeping busy sleeping with one and maybe two of the Navy SEALs who are supposed to be protecting Becky."

"What about Dwight?" Freddie asked.

"Ah, yes, Dwight. I was wondering when you were going to ask about him."

"Well?"

"It's hard to say. He appears to be the wealthy patriarch in control, except from what I can see, he isn't in control at all."

Tree finished the chicken and wiped his fingers on a napkin. "I think it's just as well you didn't marry him."

"That's your professional assessment, is it?"

"You should know that years of experience went into that conclusion," Tree said.

"Yes, I can see that. And I must say, given the man that I did marry, I would have to agree with it."

"I'm delighted to hear that," Tree said.

Freddie rose from her chair and leaned down to Tree and moved her lips close to his. "Now that you're finished eating, how would you like to accompany me into the bedroom?"

"I could do that," Tree said. "What exactly do you have in mind?"

"I'd like to spend some time reminding mself that I did in fact make the right decision."

"Yes, I believe I can help you with that," Tree said, rising to his feet and taking her in his arms.

"Then come along with me," Freddie said. "We're wasting time."

———

A dusty, unpaved county road, the sun beating down hard. What was he doing walking along a country road? Tree wondered. Under a hot, beating sun. Ahead, the road was intersected by another road, equally dusty and unpaved.

He was at a crossroads.

At the intersection of the two roads was a bench and on the bench sat a thin African-American man, an old man, his fine head shaded by a worn brown fedora. He had three-or-four-days' growth of white bristle around his chin. His khaki slacks had seen better days as had the scuffed work boots. A faded blue coat was worn over a work shirt open at the collar. As he drew closer, Tree was struck by how much the thin man looked like the actor Morgan Freeman.

"I know," said the thin man in a tired voice as Tree came to a stop. "Fellas like you always think a fella like me looks like Morgan Freeman."

"But you're not Morgan Freeman."

The man shook his head. "I only look like him—at least I look like him to you, Tree."

"How do you know my name?" Tree asked in surprise.

"Let's just say I do," said the thin man. "And let's assume that all these reports about the world coming to an end are true."

"Are they?"

The man shrugged. "World's got to come to an end sometime. Nothing goes on forever, right? So let's assume it's all over. Where does that leave you, Tree?"

"What do you mean?"

"You're soon coming face to face with your own mortality, unless I miss my guess. Death. Time to add up what you've done with your life, the pluses, the minuses. And I have to tell you, from here, those minuses, they don't look good."

"They don't?"

"How could you expect anything else, given the life you've led? The alcohol you abused, the wives you ignored, the women you chased around." The thin man mournfully shook his head. "Nope. Not good at all."

"But what about the last twelve years or so with Freddie? I love her more than anything. She changed my life, made me a better person. Doesn't that count for anything?"

"Why should it?" demanded the thin man. "You think because you stopped your drinking and carousing, you got better?"

"Yes, I guess I did, sort of," Tree said.

"Well, you didn't. Instead of staying home and nurturing your relationship with that wonderful woman, off you went on quixotic quests to justify your existence, constantly trying to get yourself killed—and at the same time placing Freddie in jeopardy. Nope. The boozing stopped, the women disappeared, but the bullets started to fly. Failing marks for your behavior, I'm sorry to say."

"I've tried my best," Tree said lamely. "I'm not perfect, not by a long shot, but I honestly tried to do better."

"Yeah, I hear that all the time," said the thin man. "But trying to do better isn't the same as *doing* better, is it?"

"What are you saying?"

"At the end, there has to be that accounting I mentioned. This is the end, time for the accounting, and you've fallen short—fallen way short…"

"No," Tree cried. "No, please. Give me another chance, there must be something I can do."

"It's a little late in the day to start changing," the thin man said, rising to his feet. He squinted up at the sun. "Time to be going." He tipped his fedora. "You take it easy now, Tree."

He started off along the road. "Wait!" Tree called after him. "There must be something I can do—there has to be!"

The thin man came to a stop at the roadside, seeming to consider what Tree had just said. He turned. "Well, okay, there is the one thing. Not that you could ever pull it off, of course."

"Give me a chance," Tree implored. "What is it?"

"You could save the world…"

"Tree." Freddie calling from a distance. No sign of her at the crossroads but he was certain he heard her.

"Tree, open your eyes…Tree…"

Tree opened his eyes. Freddie loomed over him her face etched with familiar concern. "You were having a bad dream."

"Boy, was I ever." Tree sat up slowly. Freddie held his hand. "Are you all right?"

"I think so," Tree said. "I was at a crossroads with Morgan Freeman."

"With Morgan Freeman?"

"He looked like Morgan Freeman. He said guys like me always think he looks like Morgan Freeman. He said it was time to account for my life."

"He did, huh?" Freddie was looking less worried, a little more skeptical. "That must have been interesting."

"I'm afraid Morgan didn't think I measured up."

"If it's any consolation, most of us probably don't."

"I'm a very flawed human being," Tree said.

"Yes, you are," Freddie said, moving away from the bed. "But you happen to be my flawed human being so, come on, up and at 'em."

Tree couldn't help but smile, starting to feel better.

The cellphone sounded and that brought him down to reality, thinking it must be Clint Stark calling with orders for the day.

It wasn't.

"Mr. Callister, good morning. It's Thomas. Thomas Dobbs."

Tree struggled into a sitting position. Freddie was nowhere to be seen. "What are you doing calling me at this hour?"

"It's nearly 10 o'clock, Mr. Callister. I thought for sure you'd be up by now."

"What is it, Tommy?"

"You going to be at the press conference this afternoon, aren't you?"

"I'm sorry, Tommy, I'm not at liberty to say."

"Come on, Mr. C." Tommy sounded exasperated. "Don't mess with me."

"Tommy, I told you yesterday, I can't be talking to you."

"You can't tell me what you were doing at the McPhee place last night?"

Tree was sitting up now. "How do you know where I was last night?"

"Are you kidding? We've got people staked out at the gate. Give me something, Mr. C. Anything about what happened there."

"As far as I know, nothing happened."

"Yeah, well, that's not what I hear."

"What do you hear?"

"That first thing this morning, they took the son away."

Tree was on his feet now. "What do you mean, they took him away?"

"That's what we're trying to find out. An ambulance went in there at eight o'clock and a short time later it shot back out again, sirens blazing. My guy got a glimpse of someone he thinks is Becky's younger brother, Tad."

"Obviously, I wasn't there this morning," Tree said.

"But have you heard anything?"

"Tommy, I'm standing in my bedroom. You woke me up. How would I have heard anything?"

Tree's phone began making noises that indicated another call was coming in. This time it was Clint Stark.

"Get over here—*now!*" Clint barked into the phone.

The line went dead.

12

EIGHT DAYS BEFORE THE END OF THE WORLD

If anything, the crowds surrounding the entrance gate at the McPhee compound had grown in size as Tree was ushered through by security guards who this morning greeted him with a nod and a wave—one of the boys now, a hard-bitten pro with his own gun, Kevlar vest, and two-way radio.

Well, maybe he shouldn't get too carried away with the hard-bitten part, Tree thought as he rolled up the drive and spotted Clint with Chip and Path Yoon. His band of brothers. Except the band didn't look too happy to see him after he parked and walked over to where they were gathered.

"What'd you say to Becky, you bastard?" Clint growled. Not exactly a warm welcome from a fellow brother of the band, Tree thought.

"I didn't say anything to her," Tree said.

"Someone said something because this morning she wants us gone."

"I had nothing to do with that." For once Tree didn't have any trouble sounding truthful.

"Why am I having a hard time believing you?" Chip focused narrow, suspicious eyes on Tree.

"Clint, you were there when I left last night. If I'd said something, you would have heard it."

Clint looked away as though not wanting to hear anything that sounded like logic.

"How's Tad doing?" Tree asked.

That snapped Clint around so that he was facing Tree. "Why the hell should you care?" His eyes were like a pair of small black stones.

"You know I was with Tad last night."

"An ambulance took him to hospital first thing this morning." The statement came from Chip.

"What happened to him?"

"Overdose, they think, although that's up in the air," Chip said. "Becky's pretty upset. She doesn't like the way we handled things last night."

"So the only person she wants out here is the guy least capable of offering her any protection." The unblinking black stones that were Clint's eyes never moved from Tree.

"Me?" Tree hadn't meant to sound so surprised, but that's how it came out.

"Yeah, I'm afraid so," Clint said. "Ain't that a kick in the ass?"

"Becky's dad is in there now, trying to talk some sense into her," Path said. "Let's see what happens."

Clint turned and walked away. The other two watched him worriedly. "Shit," Path Yoon said quietly. "I told him to keep it in his pants. He wouldn't listen."

"That's enough out of you," snapped Chip.

Path's otherwise neutral expression clouded with anger. "Screw you," he said. "This is all turning to shit. Thousands of crazies out there and the three of us to protect a woman who's not getting a whole lot of protection."

"You never did like her," snarled Chip.

"I never trusted her," shot back Path. "Maybe if I'd slept with her sister, I might feel differently—"

His face contorted with fury, Chip lunged at Path. "You bastard—"

Chip managed to get his hands on Path's throat before Tree stepped in to try to pull Chip away. It was like moving a rock. Then Clint was pulling the two men apart. "Settle down—both of you."

"I've had it with this prick," Chip yelled.

Tree was holding Path—not as hard to do since Path appeared to have little inclination to fight—while Clint dragged Chip away.

Everyone was frozen in place as Karen Lancaster-Simms came walking briskly from the house. "Good morning, gentlemen," she said. "Is everything all right here?"

Clint released Chip and took a deep breath. "Everything's fine, ma'am."

"You're sure about that?" Now the concern in her voice matched the expression on her face.

"Getting a couple of issues under control, that's all," Clint said. He straightened himself and came over to her. "What can we do for you ma'am?"

"I bring news from Mr. McPhee."

"Very good, ma'am."

"Mr. McPhee has decided that we should go forward with the previously planned security arrangements for this afternoon's press conference. Are you gentlemen in agreement with that?"

Clint nodded while the others murmured assent.

"After this afternoon, we can reassess our security situation," Karen continued. "But for now, let's move forward and make sure Becky is safe and secure this afternoon."

"Roger that." The way Clint said it showed no sign of enthusiasm.

As soon as Karen was back in the house, Clint addressed the others. "Okay, we have our marching orders, at least for now. Chip, you and Path will be inside. I'll accompany Becky in the Escalade."

He didn't look at Tree when he added, "Callister, you're assigned to the parking lot."

"The parking lot?"

"What part of parking lot do you not understand?"

"What am I supposed to do there?"

"Make sure no one steals a car. How's that?"

Tree gritted his teeth and nodded.

The front door opened and Dwight McPhee hobbled into the sunlight. He was followed by a grim-looking Becky, surprisingly elegant in a white linen pantsuit, her face enlivened with a touch of makeup. When she came down the steps and spotted Tree, she immediately went to him, ignoring the others.

"Mr. Callister," she said to him. "I just wanted to thank you for what you did last night, for helping Tad."

"How is he?"

"Not good, but at least he's in the hospital where he can get help."

"How are you doing?"

"I'm getting through." She clasped his hand in hers. "Thank you again."

Then, still without acknowledging the others, she turned to join her waiting father. Dwight gave Tree a look and then his daughter helped him into the Cadillac Escalade that was standing by, the motor running.

"Okay," Clint announced, "let's saddle up!"

13

Crowds, held back by tense Sanibel police officers, swarmed either side of Periwinkle Way as Clint, behind the wheel of the Range Rover, was directed into the parking lot beside the Sanibel Community House. A howl went up as the Escalade turned into the parking lot. Along the roadside men and women dressed in white robes were lined up on their knees, seeming to beseech the heavens.

The noise from the mob grew to a roar as Becky stepped out of the Escalade, her eyes—and her emotions—hidden behind large dark glasses. She turned to help her father struggle out and then started into the building, flanked by Clint and Chip, trailed closely by Path Yoon.

When they were inside, the crowd's roar diminished considerably. Left alone, and with nothing else to do, Tree leaned against the Range Rover, folding his arms, feeling stupid and embarrassed by this whole spectacle, regretting he had agreed to be part of it in company with a trio of hard muscled, squint-eyed assholes who took one look at him and saw an old man who was only going to get in the way.

As much as he resented their mindset, Tree had to admit they were right. He didn't fit in, except in a way as it turned out unexpectedly, he did—at least as far as Becky McPhee was concerned. She obviously was fed up with Clint and Chip and what she believed, rightly or not, was their infatuation with her sister.

He was, briefly, Becky's knight in shining armor, except the knight had been relegated to guarding a parking lot, swatting at no-see-ums and listening to the cicadas in the oppressive afternoon heat. Tree adjusted his sunglasses and wished he had brought water, not to mention sunblock.

"Mr. Callister." Tree pulled himself out of his reverie as Tommy Dobbs walked toward him. "I thought that was you. What are you doing here?"

"I'm guarding the parking lot, what does it look like?"

Tommy looked bemused. "Why are you guarding a parking lot?"

"To prevent anyone from stealing a car, of course. Why aren't you inside?"

"I'm on my way," Tommy said. "I was just across the street interviewing some of those religious people. They call themselves Heaven's Gate, a sect from Colorado. They believe that Becky is correct and the apocalypse will arrive with the solar eclipse. They are in white so that they will be properly dressed when they go to heaven."

"They must be confident they're going to heaven," Tree said.

"I don't get it," Tommy said. "One woman who hardly anyone had heard of before she went into space, announces that the world is ending, and everyone not only believes her but starts to go nuts."

"What about you, Tommy? Do you think the world is going to end?"

"Are you kidding? Just when I'm starting to make it big in American journalism?"

"You'd better get inside, Tommy," Tree said. "You're going to have trouble making it big if you miss the press conference."

Tommy gave Tree a sly look. "Any idea what she plans to say?"

"Nobody confides in me," Tree said. "Why do you think they've got me guarding the parking lot?"

"If you hear anything, Mr. Callister…"

"Better get inside, Tommy."

"Hey, Mr. Callister, it's Thomas, remember?"

"Right, Tommy—Thomas."

"That's better, Mr. Callister. See you later."

Tommy hurried away and the boredom set in again. On Periwinkle Way the throng began to disperse. Members of Heaven's Gate were on their feet, a surprising number of them lighting cigarettes as they mingled and chatted together. Tree spent some time considering whether members of the cult would be allowed to smoke once they reached heaven. When the smokers got to heaven and discovered there was no smoking, would they be unhappy? Would they begin to regret their enthusiasm for going to a place where you could not smoke?

"Callister…"

Tree turned, trying to see where the voice had come from.

"Callister, over here…"

Becky McPhee peered around the corner of the Community House. Startled, Tree started toward her. "Don't come over here," she called in a whispery voice.

Tree stopped, not sure what to do. "Is something wrong? Are you okay?"

"I want you to get in the Escalade and start it up. Then bring it over here. Do you understand?"

"I need the fob that starts the engine," Tree said.

"It's in the car," Becky said. "Hurry."

Tree went to the Escalade. The driver's-side door was unlocked. He got in. The engine purred to life. Tree put it in drive and eased the Escalade as close to the corner of the building as he could get it. As soon as he came to a stop, the passenger door opened and Becky hopped in.

"They think I've gone to the bathroom," she said. "Let's get the hell out of here."

14

Tree shot Becky a glance as she huddled against the passenger door. "Are you sure this is what you want to do?"

"Just be quiet and drive will you—before they realize I
didn't in fact go to the bathroom."

Tree turned onto Periwinkle.

"Where do you want to go?"

"I don't know, somewhere quiet where I don't have to deal
with all this shit for a few minutes. Can you arrange that?"

"Yes, I think I can," Tree said, not at all sure that he could.

"For what it's worth, Mr. Callister, right now you're the
only one around here I have any trust in."

"If you trust me, then call me Tree," he said.

"All right—Tree." Accompanied by the flicker of a smile.

Not sure what he was getting himself into, wondering what
the ramifications would be of her doing this and him being
complicit in it, he drove as far as Bailey Road, swung left and
then followed the road to the park at the end. He had been
there several times in the past when he needed solitude. Sure
enough, when they reached the park, it was deserted. As soon
as he brought the Escalade to a stop in the parking area, Becky
pushed open the door and shot out of the vehicle. He turned
off the motor and watched as she started along the board walkway leading to the beach.

He followed her onto the sand. She paused to remove her
shoes and then, barefoot, holding the shoes, crossed to the
surf's edge. For a moment, he thought she might walk right
into San Carlos Bay. But she went no further than the shore-

line, allowing waves to lap gently over her feet. She bent again and this time rolled up the cuffs of her linen slacks so that she could move ankle-deep into the water.

Becky stood for a time with her back to him, staring out at the bay and the hazy outline of the causeway to the right. Finally, she turned and came out of the water to where Tree waited. "I don't suppose you have a cigarette?"

"You smoke?" Tree blurted the surprised words before he could stop them.

"Don't tell NASA," she said. "When the spirit moves me or when I can convince myself that I have a good excuse. I think both those apply to the current situation. Have you got a cigarette or not?"

"Sorry," he said.

She rolled her eyes and turned away as though finished with him. Then, perhaps thinking better of it, she swung back to him. "What are you doing here?" she demanded. "I'm crazy. My family is crazy. This whole mess is crazy. But you seem sane, Tree, or sort of sane, so what the hell? Why would you ever come near us?"

"I've been asking myself the same question," Tree admitted.

"And thinking I should be put away, I imagine."

"I'm not so sure about that," Tree said honestly.

"You're not, huh? And you don't know why you're here. A great help you are." She allowed herself a smile.

Becky dropped her shoes to the sand and then removed her sunglasses to gaze around the deserted beach. "If you don't believe I'm nuts, you are part of a shrinking minority. A lot of other people think I should be put away—either that or they're as crazy as I am and believe me."

"It's a troubled time," Tree said. "Everyone's on edge. Everything seems out of whack. On top of that, an intelligent woman astronaut, a military veteran, comes back from space and announces that the world is about to end. I guess you either dismiss it as crazy or head for the hills. A lot of people appear to be heading for the hills."

"What are you going to do?"

"I'm too old for the hills," Tree said. "Besides, I've headed for them before. I've learned they don't offer much safety."

"No?"

"Nothing in them thar hills," Tree said.

That got another smile from her. A tiny victory. She said, "I know about you. More than you might think."

"You do?"

"Well, it's more accurate to say that I know about your wife. Fredryka, isn't it?"

"That's right," Tree said. "Everyone calls her Freddie."

"A long time ago, Fredryka and my father dated. But I suppose you already know that."

Tree didn't want to say he had only recently learned this. Instead, he nodded and asked, "How do you know?"

"My father told me, of course," she said with a shrug. "If I'm being honest, that may have been why he hired you—he wanted to meet you, see for himself what the man who stole away the love of his life looked like."

"Is that what Freddie was? The love of his life?"

"According to my father, yes."

"I see." Tree hoped he was putting on something resembling a brave face. "I suppose I operate under the delusion that I'm the love of her life. But who knows? Also, I had nothing to do with stealing Freddie away from your father. She was married to someone before she met me."

"Okay, but I do think something happened between them,"

Becky said. "I'm not certain what, but something more than simply dating. Do you have any idea?"

"You know, it's interesting," Tree said. "First of all, it never crossed my mind that we would have much of a chance to talk. I suppose if we did have the chance, it never occurred to me that I would be discussing the romance between my wife and the father of the world's most famous astronaut."

"But here we are, Tree, having exactly that discussion." Becky was smiling again. "For the first time in I don't know how long, I'm actually intrigued—having what resembles a human conversation that doesn't involve angry, fighting, jealous family members, or voices in space."

"Glad I could help," Tree said. "Otherwise, I don't know that I'm of much use to your father or to you."

"Believe me," she said. "You have no idea how helpful you've been."

Becky gave him something like a winsome smile—almost an apologetic smile, Tree thought. "I like you, Tree. You're my unexpected island of sanity. Can I give you a piece of advice?"

"If you want to," Tree said.

"Don't let my father take your wife away from you."

"Is that what he wants to do?"

"When my father wants something, he goes after it, and he doesn't stop until he gets it."

With that, she abruptly pivoted away heading onto the walkway.

"Hey," he called after her. "Where are you going?"

She didn't respond, just keeping walking.

"Hey," he called a minute before she was out of sight.

Tree, exasperated, started after her, reaching the walkway, confused as to what she was intending. A figure darted at him seemingly out of nowhere. He had a brief sense of someone dressed in black, a black hoodie, dark glasses hiding half his face, the other half covered by a black surgical, Covid-deterring mask.

The blow struck was like an explosion, robbing him of oxygen. Trying to breathe, the world dissolving in a painful white mist, Tree staggered off the walkway. The mist turned black. He plummeted down into the unexplored depths of his soul.

15

There were so many lights, red, blue and white, blasting at him as he tried to opened his eyes. When he finally did get them open, there was the blaze of the sun as it melted into San Carlos Bay. Too much light, making his head hurt.

The lights he discovered as he tried to sit up, were from the police and fire emergency vehicles now crowding the parking lot where he lay on a gurney beside one of the ambulances on the scene.

Then the lights were obscured by the clear face and chiseled jaw of a youthful emergency responder. "Hey, Tremain, how are we doing?"

For a second or so, Tree wasn't sure who the young responder was speaking to, but then he remembered that *he* was in fact W. Tremain Callister, and that he should respond to the responder. "What happened?"

"We were hoping you could tell us, Tremain. You've had a nasty blow to the head, possible concussion," the responder said employing the relaxed-but-in-command tone Tree was sure he had been trained to use with victims like himself.

"Someone hit me," Tree stated. He struggled to sit up causing everything around him to start spinning.

"Hey, take it easy there, partner," the first responder cautioned. "You shouldn't move around just yet."

"There was a woman with me," Tree said, trying to make the world stop turning so fast. "Is she here?"

"Sorry, Tremain, I don't know anything about a woman,

but I believe there are a couple of police officers who would like to talk to you about that."

Tree was almost sorry the merry-go-round he was on had begun to slow and then come to a stop because it brought into focus the unhappy faces of Sanibel Island police detectives Cee Jay Boone and Owen Markfield. It occurred to Tree as they approached that in all the years he had known them, he had seldom seen them smile.

And they certainly weren't smiling now. There might well be a good reason for that, Tree concluded.

"We'll take it from here," Cee Jay said to the first responder.

"Sure, but this man should go to a hospital. He took quite a bang on the noggin."

"Mr. Callister over the years has taken many head blows," Cee Jay said. "They don't seem to have had the least effect on him."

The first responder faded. The merry-go-round came to a full stop. The faces of both Cee Jay and Markfield were set in unusually dour expressions. "Tell us what happened, Tree." Cee Jay's tone was hard.

"Where's Becky McPhee? I was here with her. Where is she?"

"Becky isn't here, Tree."

"What do you mean she's not here?"

"Just what I said. Something's happened. Tell us what you know."

"With none of your usual lies and screwing around," Markfield added.

"She must be here," Tree protested. "I drove her to this beach; she was with me on the beach."

"Okay, fine," said Cee Jay. "But now she's gone, okay? When did you last see her?"

"She was here, walking back to the Escalade. I called to her and then followed her and then someone came out of nowhere and hit me. The next thing I know, I'm lying on a gurney talking to the two of you."

"What time was this?" Cee Jay asked.

"I don't know, I wasn't looking at my watch. Sometime later in the afternoon, around three, I suppose."

"Around three," Cee Jay repeated, giving Markfield a look.

"Becky might be able to tell you better," Tree said. "She must be here somewhere."

"Tree, get it through your head. Becky McPhee isn't here. She's missing."

Tree looked at her, dumbfounded. "But she was here…" was all he could say.

"Well, she's gone," Markfield interjected, barely able to contain his anger.

"What were you doing on the beach in the first place?" Cee Jay asked in a calmer voice.

"She came out of the Community House, said she wanted to get away, some place that was quiet, away from everything."

"And you brought her here?"

"In the Escalade. That's right."

"Why here?"

"I don't know," Tree said. "It was the only place I could think of that would be quiet, away from the crowds, that would be deserted at this time of the day."

"How long were you here?"

"Not long. Less than an hour."

"And how did Becky seem?"

"Anxious, I suppose, given everything that's happened to her. Once we got here, though, she seemed to relax."

"Let her guard down, I guess." Markfield sounded nasty as

he spoke. "No security, trusting someone she should never have trusted in the first place."

"What's that supposed to mean?" Tree asked angrily.

"Tree," Cee Jay said, "we can't be sure at this time but increasingly it looks as though Becky McPhee has been abducted. The person who enabled this to happen, who lured her away from her security contingent, brought her to a deserted place where she had no protection and was most vulnerable, that person was you."

"I don't understand," Tree said, trying to wrap his battered head around what he was hearing. "Who would abduct her? Who would know we were here?"

"We're hoping you might help us out with that," Cee Jay said.

"Me?" Tree said in astonishment. "How would I know?"

"Because, Mr. Tree Callister," snarled Markfield, "we suspect, given all the evidence that we've been able to piece together so far, it looks to us that you may have been complicit in the kidnapping of Becky McPhee."

16

The first responders on the scene thought Tree might have suffered a concussion and therefore should go to the hospital for further testing.

Tree decided against a hospital visit for the time being, and that gave detectives Boone and Markfield the opening they needed to transport him to Sanibel Police Headquarters and settle him into an all-too-familiar interrogation room. By then, the banging in Tree's head had subsided enough for him to realize how badly he had once again screwed things up.

Badly enough, he surmised, that not only had his carelessness allowed for the abduction of Becky McPhee, but now he was suspected of being an accomplice to that abduction. Before he could beat himself up too badly, the door opened. He expected Cee Jay or Markfield to storm in. Instead, a large woman wearing a dark suit and a matching eyepatch covering her left eye, entered carrying two bottles of water. The woman tossed Tree one of the bottles saying, "I thought you might need some water, Tree."

Tree would have liked to have demonstrated his quick reflexes by adroitly catching it, but instead he fumbled the catch and the bottle fell to the desk. The woman's good eye, an almost iridescent blue, widened a bit in—what? Surprise? Disdain?

Probably disdain, Tree concluded, retrieving the bottle. "Thanks," he said, as he twisted off the cap and took deep gulps.

"FBI Special Agent Drew Castle, Tree," the woman declared as she settled into the chair opposite Tree. She set her water down, and then ignored it to focus on Tree. "Because this is a possible kidnapping and given the seriousness of the case and its high profile, they've assigned me out of the Miami office."

"Okay," Tree said carefully.

"For now, this is simply a conversation," Drew said. "A couple of people talking. Nothing recorded. Nothing official. What do you say to that?"

"I say you're lying to me," Tree answered.

Drew Castle chuckled. "Do you now."

"Special Agent, I don't know what they told you, but I've sat in this room far too many times, enough to know that when I'm talking to an FBI agent there is no such thing as 'a couple of people talking.' Let's not waste time while you draw me out about our mutual likes and dislikes, how unlikely it is for me to be a private investigator on an island where nothing ever happens, and aren't I a little old for this, and all the other blather that, frankly, I'm tired of. Let's just get down to it."

"You left out the part where you tell me that the local detectives don't much like you, that Detective Markfield—I believe that's his name—would just as soon see you in jail."

"Actually, I think Detective Markfield would prefer to feed me to the alligators in the Everglades," Tree said.

"Well, you know him better than I do. If it's any consolation, Tree—do you mind if I call you Tree?"

"You're going to call me Tree, anyway. So go ahead, call me Tree."

"Tree, fine. If it's any consolation, I don't want to feed you to the alligators."

"Don't be too hasty," Tree said. "The night isn't over."

"I hear what you're saying. Let's forgo the chit-chat. Why don't we get started with you telling me what happened?"

"Like I repeatedly told the detectives. Becky came out of

the Sanibel Community House where she had been scheduled to give a press conference. She said she wanted out of there."

"Did she say why?" Drew asked.

Tree shook his head. "She didn't, really, other than to say she wanted to get away from what she said was 'all this shit.' The only place I could think of offhand was the beach at the end of Bailey Road. When we got there, she walked on the beach and we talked."

"What did you talk about?"

She told me I was the one she trusted."

"That's curious," Drew said. "You had just met her, hadn't you?"

"The afternoon before," Tree said.

"What made you so trustworthy?"

"I don't know, except there had been an incident involving her brother the night before."

"The night before?"

"Her brother was high on something and he had a gun. It looked as though he might shoot himself. I managed to get the gun away from him. She was appreciative of that."

"Okay, she said she trusted you, then what?"

"As I told the other officers, she suddenly turned and started back along the walkway that led to the parking lot. I followed, calling to her but she simply kept walking and didn't respond. I caught a glimpse of someone coming at me. This person struck me on the head and that's when I lost consciousness."

"That's it?" Drew made it sound as though there had to be more.

"That's it," Tree said with a shrug. "When I regained consciousness, there were all sorts of police and fire, and Becky was gone."

"Gone…" Drew appeared to be digesting the word as she

sat back to get a better view of her suspect. "Okay, I've got the bare bones of your story, and that's fine. But your thinking during all this Tree, I'm not sure what your thinking was."

"Thinking about what?"

"Given her notoriety, given the security concerns, what you thought about driving Ms. McPhee anywhere unsupervised, unprotected."

"I was with her. She was distraught, insistent. What was I supposed to do?"

"What were you *supposed* to do?" Drew's voice had taken on a hard tone. "What you were supposed to do is keep her safe—ensure that Ms. McPhee was surrounded by the professionals who were hired to protect her. You were not supposed to put her in a vulnerable place where she wasn't protected at all."

"Except she wasn't happy with her security team," Tree said.

"But she was happy to go to a deserted beach with you, an untrained amateur?"

"I don't believe she was thinking like that," Tree said.

Drew's one good eye narrowed. "Then, there is that other possibility, isn't there, Tree?"

"What do you mean?"

"Let me tell you what my team is thinking about this. They are considering the possibility that this whole thing was carefully orchestrated, that you are part of a plot to kidnap Becky McPhee."

"That's insane," Tree said.

"You know what, Tree?" Drew sat back in her chair. "Strangely enough, I agree with you. I'll tell you why. Meeting you this evening, I'd have to say at first blush you're too old and too much of an amateur to pull off something like a kidnapping. But could you be a knowing pawn in someone else's game? Yeah, that's definitely a possibility." She leaned forward, her elbows on the table. "But you gotta help me, my friend. Give me something, anything, that will lead us to Ms. McPhee."

Tree thought about it and then said, "The only thing that stands out is Becky suddenly walking away from me a moment before I was attacked."

"Okay. Why does that stand out?"

"One minute we were talking—she said something about me never knowing how much I had helped her—and then she was disappearing along the boardwalk leading to the parking lot. I called to her, but she didn't respond, kept walking. That's when I was attacked…"

"Before this happened, what were you talking about?"

"Curiously enough, we talked about my wife, Freddie."

"Why would Becky talk about your wife?"

"A long time ago, before we met, Freddie dated Becky's father in Chicago."

Drew looked surprised. "That's what you were talking about?"

"Briefly, yeah. She said that's how she knew me."

"Did you know about this? About your wife dating Dwight McPhee?"

"My wife had recently told me."

Drew paused, taking in what Tree had just told her. "Okay, speaking of relationships, she didn't happen to mention someone named Valentin Baturin?"

"No," Tree said. "Who's he?"

"Valentin Baturin. He's nicknamed Bear."

"I have no idea who that is and she never said anything about a guy named Bear."

"Okay." Drew was on her feet, seeming to have suddenly lost interest in talking further to Tree.

"Okay?" Tree said. "Now what?"

"Now you sit there until we figure out what to do with you."

"That wasn't much of a conversation," Tree said.

"And you're not much of a liar."

"I'm not lying," Tree said.

"Aren't you? Well, that remains to be seen."

Drew started for the door. Tree called after her. "What about Valentin Baturin? You didn't tell me who he is. Who is he?"

Drew didn't answer. When she reached the door, she turned. "Just so you know, Tree…"

"What?"

"Becky's brother, Tad, died in hospital a couple of hours ago."

17

Time passed. Tree's head began hurting again. He drank his water and thought about Tad McPhee waving that gun around in the night, wanting to kill himself. Had he finally succeeded? Evidently, he was not willing to wait around to see if his sister was right about the end of the world.

How long had he been sitting here? An hour? Tree looked at his watch. Nearing eight o'clock.

He hated this. He knew what they were doing, sweating him out in a dingy interrogation room, leaving him to stew in his own thoughts, reaching the point where, in desperation, he would spill the beans.

Except there weren't any beans to spill. At least he didn't think there were.

He thought of Becky talking about Freddie and her father. What was that about? Was it anything? Tree had enough time on his hands to feel another twinge of unexpected jealousy. He thought again about why Becky might bring that up. And what about someone named Valentin Baturin? The name must be important to the FBI, but why?

The door opened, interrupting his thoughts. Tree jerked to attention, half expecting someone with a rubber hose. Instead, T. Emmett Hawkins came through the door armed not with a rubber hose, but a frown—the frown he usually wore like a comfortable suit of clothes whenever he had to deal with Tree. As usual, Tree was only too glad to see him.

"One of these days, Tree," Hawkins said, "it would be nice to meet up with you when you are not in police custody." He spoke with that reassuring honeyed drawl he affected when dealing with clients tormented by nightmares of authorities throwing keys away.

"I would like that, Emmett," Tree said.

"Unfortunately, this is not to be one of those occasions." Emmett's voice was full of sad resignation.

"I suppose it isn't," Tree said. "How did you know I was here?"

Emmett offered the approximation of a smile. "Keeping in mind our lamentable history together, I should say something like, 'where else would you be?' But I will forgo snide comments because it's getting late. Suffice to say your wonderful, supportive wife who could do much better, incidentally, got in touch with me. She's waiting outside. You, Tree, are a very lucky man."

"As far as Freddie is concerned, I am. Very lucky. As far as the rest of it goes, I'm not so sure. How much trouble am I in?"

"I've had occasion to speak with the local police and the FBI agents who have been brought in on what they suspect is a kidnapping case and therefore under their jurisdiction. I'm left with the impression they would like nothing better than to throw a rope over a tree branch with you on the end of it. However, I have prevailed upon them, and for the time being they are willing to release you from custody."

"Do they really believe I masterminded a plot to kidnap Becky McPhee?"

"Hardly the mastermind," Hawkins said. "Don't take this personally, Tree, but the thinking is you don't have the brains to participate very effectively in a kidnapping plot, therefore they are for the moment anyway, ruling you out as suspect—somewhat reluctantly, I must say."

"I should be offended," Tree said.

"Don't be. Otherwise, you would be in jail tonight."

"Well, thanks, Emmett," Tree said, beginning to rise to his feet.

"There is a slight complication."

That stopped Tree halfway out of his seat. "A *slight* complication?"

"I've agreed to bring you and Freddie to Becky's father, Dwight McPhee—he'd like to talk to you."

"Well, that's not a problem," Tree said. "I'd like to talk to him. Besides, my car is at his place."

"You know his son passed this afternoon?"

"Yes, the FBI told me."

"Did they tell you the death is being investigated as a homicide?"

"No, they didn't."

"Just so you're prepared when we get there," Hawkins said. "Now, one more thing. A herd of press lurks outside. The police are suggesting we go out the back, and I'm saying do that because I don't want you shooting off your mouth and getting yourself into even more trouble."

"I promise to be quiet," Tree said.

"Oh, if only that were possible," Hawkins said with a roll of his eyes.

The rear of the police building was, as Hawkins predicted, deserted except for Freddie, spectacular in jeans and a linen jacket, arms folded, stationed beside Hawkins' Lincoln Continental. It would not be accurate to say that at the sight of Tree, she rushed into his arms. Rather, she approached tentatively, as though uncertain whether to embrace her husband or kill him. She did neither. Instead, she posed a question asked far too many times over the past decade, "Are you all right?"

"A little banged up, that's all," Tree replied.

"You're always 'a little banged up.'"

"I'm sorry," he said. "This is the last thing I expected."

"Unfortunately, I've come to expect the last thing you expected," Freddie said.

She embraced him then, burying her head against his shoulder, murmuring, "Madness, this is madness." She pulled away to look at him. "You do realize what's happened?"

Tree shook his head. "I don't know anything. I've been locked in a police interrogation room."

"Horror and shock," Freddie stated. "The astronaut who fell to earth to announce the end of the world has disappeared. And guess who is at the center of it all?" She didn't wait for an answer. "My husband."

Before Tree had a chance to say anything, the back door of the police station banged open and Detective Owen Markfield shot out, his face set in fury. He charged across the pavement, fists curled, alarming enough that T. Emmett Hawkins felt compelled to speedily step in front of Tree as though to shield him from what appeared certain to be Markfield's incoming blows.

The sight of the diminutive Hawkins resplendent in his bow tie, shoulders hunched, tensed protectively in front of his client, stopped Markfield short of his prey. Hands clenched in fists, he breathed like an enraged bull.

"This isn't over, you son of a bitch!" he yelled.

It was not hard to guess which of the three of them Markfield was addressing.

"My suggestion, Detective Markfield is that you take a deep breath, and restrain yourself," Hawkins said soothingly, in a way that would make an invading army think twice about the attack. "Any aggressive action on your part will take place with an attorney present and will only create problems that you probably don't need."

That had the effect of settling Markfield, transforming him so that he was less the heavy breathing bull, more a simple homicidal maniac pointing a threatening finger. "They shouldn't be letting you out of here, you bastard! They think you're a careless nitwit who doesn't know what he's doing. But I know better, Callister. You know where that woman is and you're up to your ears in this—I don't know how, but you're involved and if it's the last thing I do, I'm going to nail your ass."

"Tree and Freddie," Hawkins said, keeping the honey in his voice at a reasonable level, "go ahead and get into my car."

Freddie got in the back while Tree slid into the passenger seat. They watched through the windshield as Hawkins, seemingly vulnerable in the face of Markfield's coiled intensity, stepped close to the detective. The words he spoke had the effect of making Markfield abruptly turn on his heel and storm back into police headquarters.

Hawkins, his clear unlined face revealing nothing, sauntered to the Lincoln and slipped behind the wheel. "Let us be off," he said as the car's V8 engine growled to life.

"What did you say to Markfield?" Tree asked.

Hawkins produced one of the Cheshire-cat smiles for which he had become famous in South Florida. "Let's simply say he knows where I'm coming from."

18

The big white television production trucks that had become ubiquitous on the island already lined the street across from the McPhee compound. Sanibel police and sheriff's deputies were on duty, holding back the reporters and cameramen. The crowd of onlookers was swelling to the point where the police had to clear a path so that Hawkins could guide the Lincoln through a front gate now secured by a half dozen security guards in Kevlar vests, carrying automatic weapons. The area surrounding the main house was as bright as day thanks to the floodlights that had been set up around the periphery.

Everything was in place to protect someone who wasn't there, Tree reflected as one of the guards approached, finger on the trigger of his weapon. Hawkins said, "I'm T. Emmett Hawkins. Mr. McPhee has asked to see my client, Mr. Tree Callister."

"You're expected, sir," the guard said, nodding for Hawkins to go ahead. He came along the drive, slowing as he reached the main house where more armed security people were stationed, among them a grim Clint Stark.

After Hawkins parked and the three of them got out, caught in the glare of the floodlights, Clint walked over and announced peremptorily, "Mr. McPhee is waiting for you. I'll take you inside."

Tree caught Freddie out of the corner of his eye. She had turned pale. "Are you okay?"

She took a deep breath and nodded. "It's been a long time, that's all."

What did that mean? But then Clint was leading the trio inside and there was no more time for rumination because Karen Lancaster-Simms had appeared with Dwight McPhee. To Tree's eyes, Dwight looked handsome as the devil, elegantly leaning on his cane, fixing an uncertain smile.

"Hello, Fredryka," Karen said. "I'm Karen Lancaster-Simms, I work for Mr. McPhee. It's a pleasure to meet you."

Freddie, uncharacteristically, said nothing, simply giving a nod of recognition.

Clint Stark stayed put and was soon joined by Chip Holbrook and Path Yoon. All three focused hard eyes on Tree, ready in case he decided to attack. Tree couldn't bring himself to point out they were ready for the wrong guy. Instead, he watched Dwight's expression as he greeted Freddie—his long-lost love? From the look on Dwight's face, you could be forgiven for believing that.

Karen was saying, "And I believe you already know Mr. McPhee."

"It's been a long time, Fredryka," Dwight said.

"I'm so sorry about what's happened," Freddie said, showing genuine concern. "I understand your son passed away this afternoon."

"Sad to say," responded Dwight, lowering his head to acknowledge his loss. Then he brightened. "But it is good to see you again, even under these terrible circumstances. And I must say, you haven't changed much; you look as lovely as ever."

He turned to Tree, his expression much less welcoming. "Tree, how are you feeling?"

Tree nodded and said, "I'm sorry about Tad."

"Yes, thank you, but right now, we must focus on Becky and what's happened to her."

"I understand." He turned to Hawkins. "Dwight, do you know T. Emmett Hawkins?"

"Only by reputation," Dwight said, dragging his eyes away from Freddie and focusing on Hawkins. "How do you do, sir? I won't shake your hand, given the time we're in. I presume you are here to make sure we don't beat Tree to a pulp."

Hawkins allowed a watery smile. "Let me simply say that earlier I was able to play a part in helping Tree navigate his latest encounter with the authorities."

"I'm hoping Tree won't need a lawyer to get him through this visit," Dwight said.

"I can't imagine that's the case," Hawkins replied. But he didn't offer to wait outside, Tree noticed.

"I think everyone will be much more comfortable in the other room," Karen suggested. "Why don't I lead the way?"

No one objected.

They settled into a high-ceilinged great room cast in gloom, as though in mourning for the missing Becky and the deceased Tad. Karen directed the visitors onto chairs and sofas and then oversaw Dwight as he sank into an armchair not far from Freddie and Tree. She cast a wary glance at Freddie before moving to position herself near the three former Navy SEALs filling the background, tense and stern, ready for anything. Being ready for anything came a little late, Tree thought.

"Naturally, my concern tonight is for my daughter," Dwight began. He addressed Tree: "If there's anything you can tell us, Tree, that will help us understand what happened...."

"Like what the hell you thought you were doing," Clint interjected.

"Clint, that's enough," Dwight said. "It's important that we all remain calm so we can work this through."

"I thought I was helping someone in obvious distress," Tree

explained. "I don't know what happened at the press conference, but Becky was determined to get away…"

"That's the thing," Dwight said. "Nothing happened. She
excused herself to go to the bathroom and a few minutes later,
when she didn't come back, that's when we all realized, she was
gone."

Clint couldn't resist a glare at Tree. "And then it turns out
that Callister in his infinite wisdom decided to drive her away
without thinking to tell me or anyone else. Jesus."

Dwight raised a calming hand. "Okay, I understand emotions are running high, but let's give Tree a chance here. Please,"
he said, "tell us from your perspective what happened, Tree."

As he had with the police and the FBI, Tree once again
described Becky's unexpected appearance in the parking lot,
her insistence that he drive her away, their arrival at the beach,
the attack by the masked and hooded intruder, waking up with
an aching head surrounded by police and emergency workers.

When Tree finished, Dwight turned to the hovering Clint.
"Any questions, Captain Stark?"

"Frankly, I'm having the same trouble with Callister's story
as the cops," Clint said. "If none of this was planned, how did
the kidnappers know that you were at the beach?"

"The people who took her must have followed us from the
Community House," Tree said.

Clint nodded and then said, "But then how did they know
Becky was going to leave the press conference in the first place?
And further, how could they know she was going to get into a
vehicle and drive off with you?"

"They couldn't know, is the short answer," Tree replied.
"They may have been as surprised as I was—saw an opportu-
nity and took it."

"Any way you cut it, all this is hard to swallow," Clint said.

"Somehow Becky ends up on a deserted beach with the newest member of the team, the old guy least able to counter any attack."

Tree ignored the jibe and focused on Dwight. "You say nothing happened at the press conference. Are you sure?"

"Yes, I think so," Dwight said. "There was a lot of noise, hot lights, reporters clamoring to ask questions, chaotic I suppose would be the best way to describe it. But Becky knew what she was getting into; she said she wanted to clear the air, get it over with and be done with it. She was expecting the press to be hostile and I would say the questions reflected that."

"Fake news bastards," Clint muttered.

"She said she wanted to clear the air," Tree said. "What did she mean by that?"

"She didn't really have much of chance to say anything," Dwight said. "Karen introduced her and that was followed by a cacophony of press questions, then Becky got up and excused herself."

"How long was it before Becky left?" Tree asked.

Dwight shrugged. "I wasn't paying much attention to the time. But not long. Maybe fifteen, twenty minutes." Dwight looked at Clint. "Does that sound right to you, Captain?"

"Yeah, about twenty minutes," Clint said.

Path Yoon abruptly stepped forward. "There was that woman," he said.

"What about her?" Tree asked. He noticed Clint scowl at Path.

"Yes, that was the one question that Becky answered before she left," Karen said stepping forward. "I don't know about the rest of you but I was surprised when Becky responded in Russian."

Tree looked at Dwight. "Becky speaks Russian?"

"She does," Dwight said. "She's not fluent, but she knows enough to get by. That was one of the reasons NASA wanted her on the space station, so she could communicate with her Russian counterparts."

"Any idea what the Russian reporter asked or how Becky responded?"

Dwight shook his head.

"But right after that," Path added, "Becky excused herself to go to the bathroom."

"Valentin Baturin," Tree said. "Would the reporter's question have had anything to do with him?"

Dwight's face reflected confusion. "I have no idea."

"Do you know who he is?"

"Vaguely. He's a Russian cosmonaut. Originally, he was to be on the space station, but something happened and he didn't go on the mission."

"Any idea why?"

Dwight again shook his head. "Why the questions about Baturin?"

"The FBI asked me about him," Tree said.

"And what did you say?"

"I said I have no idea who he is."

The room fell to silence, soon broken by T. Emmett Hawkins. "If there's nothing else, I propose that it's late and we are all tired, and that we call it a night."

He punctuated the suggestion by rising to his feet. Tree was about to follow when Dwight's daughter, Miranda, lurched into the room. She was dressed in jean shorts and a blouse open almost to the waist. She held a tumbler of dark liquid.

"It's all bullshit," she announced loudly, swaying back and forth, her full mouth fitted with a crooked smile.

"Miranda—" Dwight grew tense, speaking in a warning voice.

Miranda's blurry gaze fell on Tree. "Don't listen to any of their bullshit. My brother's dead. Someone killed him, okay? They will tell you differently, but they're lying. You were there, you tried to help him. I heard that. He was out of it, but okay. Next thing, he's dead…*shit!*"

"Miranda!" Dwight was leaning hard on his cane, struggling to his feet. "Stop this!"

"They're trying to set you up," she said to Tree. "They're trying to make it look as though you're responsible for my sister's disappearance. They don't want anyone to know what's really going on."

Dwight, standing now, clutched at his daughter. She yanked away, spilling her drink. Clint lunged, plucking the glass out of her hand.

As Clint took hold of her, Miranda called out, "Be careful… they're bastards—don't trust them. They're liars and murderers—"

Dwight's face had twisted into fury. He called out, "Chip! Help the captain. Get her the hell out of here. Now!"

As Chip moved to Clint's aid, Miranda shrank away, screaming, "Leave me alone you bastards! Leave me alone!"

Part of Navy SEALs training must have involved lessons on how to control semi-hysterical drunks. Clint had managed to adroitly wrap his arms around Miranda so that as she continued to scream blue murder, he frog-marched her out of the room, Chip following. Path Yoon, Tree noticed, stayed put, unmoving, his face showing nothing.

"I'm so very sorry, Fredryka," Dwight said to Freddie.

"It's fine, Dwight," Freddie said. "This is all very sad and everyone's under a great deal of stress."

"A nightmare." Dwight's voice was breaking. "I don't know what to make of it, I really don't."

"What Miranda was saying…" Tree interjected.

"It's nonsense…liars, murderers," Dwight said angrily. "Why…why would she say things like that at a time like this?"

"Miranda's had too much to drink," Karen said, moving to Dwight. "You know what she's like when she gets like this."

Karen maneuvered herself between Tree and Dwight as if to physically block further questioning. "I think we've all had enough for tonight."

"Yes, yes, I think you're right," Dwight said distractedly.

Dwight gave Freddie what looked to Tree like a longing glance before he seemed to deflate. "Thank you all for coming. For trying to help…"

He turned and hobbled out of the room. The last thing Tree saw as he exited with Freddie and Hawkins was Clint Stark shooting him the kind of piercing look that Tree imagined was on a Navy SEAL's face just before he slit the throat of a terrorist.

And Tree wasn't even a terrorist. Or maybe in Clint's books, he was.

19

"How is your head?" Freddie asked once they had arrived at Andy Rosse Lane.

Tree was sprawled on the living room sofa, Freddie nearby nursing the glass of chardonnay that, after the day's events, she certainly needed.

"Still hurting," Tree said.

"We should get you to the hospital."

"If it isn't better in the morning, but right now it's manageable."

"A head that has been hit many, many times," Freddie said. "An exceptionally hard head. A curious head. A head that can take the blows but doesn't allow for any rational thinking."

"In my defense, I would say I don't know how I could have avoided what happened today," Tree said.

"No? Well, I can think of a number of ways," Freddie replied. "But right now, I'm going to keep my mouth shut."

"You haven't told me what you thought seeing Dwight McPhee again."

"He's in a shaky emotional state, that's for sure. A son dead, his daughter missing. Another daughter drunk. He's got a lot to deal with."

"When we were at the beach, Becky told me that you are the love of her father's life. He's never gotten over you, according to her."

"Becky told you that?"

"That was more or less all we talked about before I got hit on the head and she disappeared."

"If that's the case, and I wonder if it is, Dwight certainly remembers things a lot differently than I do."

"How do you remember—*things?*"

Freddie gave him another in the long series of disbelieving looks she had delivered to Tree over the years. "Why are we talking about this when we should be talking about what happened to you today?"

"Such as my involvement in the conspiracy to kidnap the woman who has predicted the end of the world?"

"Yes, we could certainly talk about that."

"At the same time, I can't help but wonder if that might somehow be connected to your relationship with Dwight McPhee."

"My very long-ago relationship—and how could that possibly be connected to his daughter's disappearance?"

"I don't know," Tree admitted.

"What about Dwight's other daughter—"

"Miranda."

"Drunken Miranda. What she said about you being set up."

"But set up by whom? Her father? That doesn't make sense."

"Also, this Russian cosmonaut you asked about."

"Valentin Baturin. That's because the FBI asked me about him, although they didn't say he was a Russian cosmonaut who had been at the space station."

"Putting aside the fact that she was drunk, Miranda does appear to believe her father is up to something."

"Either that or Miranda doesn't like her family and doesn't think I should be anywhere near them. I tend to agree with her."

"Meanwhile," Freddie added, "the FBI, not to mention your pal Owen Markfield, seems to suspect that you know a whole lot more than you're letting on."

"As far as the feds are concerned, they do and they don't. On the one hand they have their suspicions, on the other hand they think I am too old and dumb to pull off something like this."

"I don't know about too old…"

"Hey," Tree said in mock horror.

"Only kidding," Freddie amended. "But in this case, maybe it's just as well."

"They underestimate me. That's why it's going to come as a big surprise when I fool them all."

"How do you plan to do that?" Freddie asked doubtfully.

Tree remained silent. This time Freddie chose perplexed from the many looks she could shoot her husband at times like this. "Tree…"

"What?"

"What are you thinking?"

"I'm not sure what I'm thinking," Tree replied with what he hoped was a disarming smile. "But I am thinking."

"Then there could only be trouble ahead," Freddie said with a groan.

Tree was saved from having to offer reassurances that even he wouldn't believe by a knock on the door. Not that a knock on the door at that time of night would likely be anything but more trouble.

Sure enough, when Tree opened the door, he found Tommy Dobbs standing there.

"Tommy," Tree groaned.

"Thomas, Mr. Callister. Sorry to bother you at this time of night."

"Then don't," Tree snapped.

"Come on, Mr. Callister, let me talk to you for just a couple of minutes, okay?"

"Tommy—Thomas, I don't know anything," Tree lied.

"I know you have to say that, but I know differently, okay?"

"No, you don't," Tree maintained, beginning to wonder what Tommy might know.

"The thing is, I saw you in the parking lot, just before the press conference. You said you were guarding the cars."

"That's right," Tree said.

"I'm inside and the press conference starts and then a few minutes into it, Becky McPhee says she needs to be excused, gets up and leaves. We all sit there for the next twenty-five minutes or so, watching her father and the security people grow increasingly nervous. Then it begins to dawn on a few of us in the press that Becky isn't coming back—that she's taken off."

"Tommy, it's late, I'm dead tired, what's this all about?"

"I rushed out to the parking lot because I know you're there and you probably saw what happened. Only, guess what? You're not there. Becky's gone and so are you. That could mean only one thing, Mr. Callister."

"What's that, Tommy?"

"You drove off with Becky, you know what happened— what happened, Mr. Callister? You drove off with her and now she's disappeared and the whole world is looking for her."

"What are you saying, Tommy? Are you accusing me of kidnapping Becky McPhee?"

"Of course not, Mr. Callister. But the police and the FBI thinks she was kidnapped. I think you drove her away from the Community House. So then where did you two go and what happened?"

"I can't say anything."

"But that's what went down, right?"

"Like I said, Tommy, I can't—"

"But you're not denying that's what occurred. I'll leave your name out of it, I'll say she was driven away from the press conference and that's when she disappeared. I won't be wrong if I say that, will I?"

"Good night, Tommy." Tree started to close the door. Then he had a thought. "The Russian," he said to Tommy.

"The Russian?" Tommy looked confused.

"Apparently there was a Russian reporter. She asked Becky a question and Becky replied in Russian."

"Yeah, I remember that," Tommy said uncertainly. "What's that got to do with anything?"

"Find out about that reporter, and get back to me. Maybe then I can help you."

"All right," Tommy said. "I'll see what I can find out. But in the meantime, Mr. Callister, just shake your head if anything I've said to you is wrong. Okay? A shake of the head, that's all I'm asking."

Tree closed the door.

20

SEVEN DAYS BEFORE THE END OF THE WORLD

What have you done with poor Becky McPhee?" Rex de-manded after Freddie dropped Tree off at the Cattle Dock Bait Company the next morning.

"A question I was asked many times yesterday," Tree said, settling behind his desk, still dead tired and still experiencing a sore head and various aching body parts.

"The telephone has been ringing off the proverbial hook all morning," Rex said. "I keep thinking it's the *New York Times* asking to interview me for my new book. Instead, it's every reporter under the sun wanting to talk to you."

"They are not supposed to know I'm involved," Tree said.

"Well, they do," Rex said.

"I'm not involved."

"Bullshit," Rex stated. "You're involved."

"But thanks for running interference, Rex."

"It's the sad story as my life fades to an end," Rex said. "Have you watched CNN this morning?"

"I'm not watching CNN," Tree said.

"That's why everyone is calling. Their correspondent, your old pal Tommy Dobbs, is reporting that you are a person of interest in what they are now calling an abduction. A lovely phrase for accusing you of a crime without actually accusing you of the crime. According to your pal Tommy—"

"He's not my pal," Tree interjected grumpily.

"According to Tommy, you're the member of Becky's security team who drove her away from the Community House just before she was kidnapped. Is that true?"

"I'm not saying anything," Tree said.

"Good grief," Rex said, "it *is* true."

Gladys arrived at that moment. "I just heard on NPR that you are a person of interest," she said to Tree. "That doesn't sound very good."

"It's not good at all," agreed Rex.

"I'm surprised there aren't reporters and cameras all over the place," Gladys said.

"If it's any consolation to the two of you, the FBI thinks I don't have the intelligence to be involved in a plot to kidnap Becky McPhee."

"Sounds like damn fine investigative police work," Rex said dryly.

"I hate to disagree with a crack body of law enforcement like the FBI," Gladys said. "But I do believe Tree is smart enough to be involved in a kidnapping plot, although I hasten to add, Tree, I can't imagine you are."

"Thanks for that," Tree said. "The FBI also thinks I'm too old."

"Well," Gladys said, "there is that."

"What?" said Rex indignantly. "You get to a certain age and you can't kidnap anyone?"

"What are you going to do?" Gladys asked Tree.

"My advice is that you do nothing," Rex interjected. "Whenever you do anything, big trouble follows."

"There's a guy named Valentin Baturin."

"What about him?" Gladys asked, seating herself at her desk.

"His name keeps coming up. Apparently, he's a Russian cosmonaut."

Gladys was at her laptop, fingers moving quickly over the keyboard. "Yup, Wikipedia's got him. Russian cosmonaut, former fighter pilot, flew on the Soyuz TM-9 that docked at the space station. His friends call him Bear. Doesn't say why." She read silently for a couple of minutes. "Interesting. He was assigned by the Russians as a liaison person at the Kennedy Space Center, but then left last year under what Wikipedia says were "unexplained circumstances."

"What are unexplained circumstances?" asked Rex.

"Those are circumstances that aren't explained—therefore are of interest to people like ourselves." Gladys looked over at Tree. "I can't see anything that links Valentin with Becky, except that they were both on the space station."

"But it doesn't sound as though they were there at the same time."

Gladys kept her focus on the computer screen while she typed some more. "Nope. He was on the space station a couple of years ago. Before Becky's time, obviously."

"Doesn't mean they don't know each other," piped in Rex.

"Is there someone around who can help us when it comes to Russians?" Gladys asked.

Tree and Rex exchanged glances, communicating an unspoken answer: There *was* someone who knew all about Russians—whether she was willing to help was another matter entirely.

21

As Gladys drove him in her pickup truck, Tree reflected yet again on the wildly unexpected fortunes of the former Judith Blair, the everyday young Chicago housewife who had married an equally young reporter.

It wasn't long before she learned to her unending disappointment, that her new husband preferred hanging out with fellow reporters in various local watering holes to coming home at night. She had never forgiven him for that transgression, and, in truth, each time he encountered Judy, he never forgave himself either. He had been a jerk, no question about it, and no apologies would change her view of him as—well, asshole might be a more appropriate description than mere jerk, at least as far as Judy was concerned.

For years, and through three subsequent marriages, Tree heard nothing from Judy. He did not exist in her life; she was gone from his. Then, to his astonishment, she turned up on Sanibel married to a Russian oligarch named Alexei Markov. To his further astonishment, when Alexei died of a heart attack, instead of fading away to the quiet life of a rich widow, Judy had, with ruthless determination and efficiency, taken control of her late husband's wide-ranging and, some would say, legally suspect business interests.

Gladys was impressed by what she could see of the Coconut Drive house through the steel gate, beyond the ten-foot wall. "This confirms my view that the rich are all hiding behind walls, in case the peasants show up with pitchforks," Gladys said.

"Or, in this case, ex-husbands," Tree said.

"Are you sure you don't want me to come in with you?"

"I stand a better chance if I'm alone—I think," Tree said.

"I hope you know what you're doing."

"My wife expresses the same hope all the time," Tree said. "In fact, all four of my wives have said that to me at one time or another."

"It does suggest that, in fact, you don't know what you're doing."

"It does, doesn't it?" Tree said. He opened the passenger door and started out. "Wish me luck."

"I suspect you're going to need it," Gladys said.

Unlike Tree's previous visits to Judy's place, this time there were no gun-toting security guards, at least none that he could see as he pressed the intercom. For a time that produced nothing. Similarly, there was no movement from the other side of the locked gates.

He pressed again. And waited.

Finally, a voice whose irritation could not be hidden by the electronic static said, "Go away, Tree."

"Come on, Judy," Tree said. "I'm here on foot. Let me in."

"Buy a car," Judy snapped.

"As soon as I resolve a few outstanding issues, that's what I intend to do."

"Outstanding issues, yes. I see you're back in the news. You're toxic, Tree. Quit showing up here every time you get into trouble. You waste my time. You only escape one mess to get into another. It's an endless cycle."

"Right now, I need your help. Please. For old time's sake. Let me in."

"God help me," said the electronic voice.

A moment later, the gates swung open with an impressive

silence, allowing Tree up the drive toward the mansion on the edge of San Carlos Bay occupied by the Judy that Tree never would have expected in a million years.

Armed bullet-headed thugs now materialized as he reached the steps leading to the front doors. Any thoughts Tree might have had about Judy reaching a point in her new life where she didn't need protection had evaporated.

One of the bullet-heads, this one identifiable by his tiny tadpole-shaped eyes, looked as though he would think nothing of killing Tree before lunch. He spoke into his sleeve before giving Tree the go ahead to enter the house. "Mrs. Markov awaits you," he said in a guttural accent that suggested ancestors on Russian steppes.

Yes, Mrs. Markov would be awaiting him, all right. If one of her security guards wouldn't knock him off, Tree suspected the waiting Mrs. Markov would cheerfully take on the job herself.

A smiling maid who actually appeared glad to see him and may have been the only unarmed member of the staff, led Tree along a wide corridor with the familiar floor-to-ceiling windows showing off a spectacular view of San Carlos Bay. Tree trailed into the unfamiliar depths of the house. The maid opened a pair of oak doors and indicated that Tree should go through.

Tree found himself in a library that might have been transplanted from *Downton Abbey* or what an American multimillionaire might have imagined was at *Downton Abbey*, with lots of dark wood and bookshelves mounted on two tiers around the room. The lower tier was mostly filled with books. Tree noticed there were a lot empty shelves in the upper tier.

"Not *Downton Abbey* if that's what you were thinking," Judy announced from a sofa where she sat cast in shafts of sunlight from the arched windows stationed between the bookshelves.

"That's what I was thinking," Tree admitted.

"I've always known what you're thinking, Tree. That was part of the problem, wasn't it? You could never put anything over on me."

Tree couldn't disagree, but for now he decided silence was the best course of action.

"Actually, if I'm being honest, the inspiration is Henry Higgins," Judy said, rising from the sofa.

"In *My Fair Lady*," Tree said.

"Ever since I was a kid, I longed for a library like the one Henry Higgins has in the movie," she said. "Now I have it."

"You need a few more books," Tree said.

"They're coming," she said.

Aha, Tree thought. Judy didn't read books; she ordered them. And today, Judy didn't so much come to him as she floated in a swirl of white caftan, an angel of a certain age, aglow with the rosy skin acquired when you have a lot of money and you can afford the people who will work on you until you take on Judy's radiance. The radiance appeared to have erased most of the wrinkles from her round face—or was it the genius of Florida's renowned plastic surgeons?

Judy floated to a stop. The sweetness that her face was now designed to contain, spoiled by having to gaze at her ex-husband. "I'm probably out of my mind for letting you in here, considering what happened the last time I was forced to deal with you."

"But you know why I'm here," Tree said. "That's why you let me in. You couldn't resist."

"Don't kid yourself, Tree. I can always resist you."

"I always know what you're thinking," Tree said.

"Bull," Judy snapped. "You never *cared* what I was thinking. Why are you here? You're here for the same reason you're always here—you're in trouble. This time it's Becky McPhee. I hear they think you helped kidnap her, and isn't that a hoot? If that's the sum total of their thinking, then I'm afraid Ms. McPhee is doomed."

"Maybe you could tell that to the FBI," Tree said.

"If you're looking for help with the feds, I'm not much use to you. They don't like you, but they like me even less."

"They kept asking me if I know someone named Valentin Baturin."

Judy waited longer than Tree might have expected before she spoke. "And what did you say when they asked you that?"

"I said I had no idea, but I would bet that my pal Judy Markov with her Russian connections, I bet she would know."

"Ha, ha," Judy said mirthlessly.

"However, I have since learned that Valentin is a cosmonaut who was on the space station, although not at the same time as Becky McPhee."

"Yes, Valentin is a cosmonaut, you got that part right."

"Then you know him?"

"I know his uncle better."

"His uncle? How do you know him?"

Instead of answering, Judy turned away from Tree, spending some time staring up at the empty shelves. "You're right," she said. "We do need more books in here."

She turned back to him that rosy round face now crumpled with irritation. "You bastard, you're determined to get me into the shit, aren't you?"

"Because I ask you for a name?"

"In my business, dealing with the people I deal with, that's sometimes all it takes."

"Asking about Valentin's uncle, for example?"

"Valentin's uncle who can get us both killed."

"Who is he?"

She thought about this before exhaling and making a noise that sounded like resignation. "Georgi Zhukov. There you go. A name—Georgi Zhukov. Now get the hell out of my sight."

"He's Valentin's uncle? Georgi Zhukov? How is a name supposed to help me?"

"It won't help you, other than to explain why Valentin suddenly was booted out of the space program."

"Because of his uncle?"

"That and the fact that Valentin was screwing Becky, and given his family background, I don't imagine NASA felt that was good for its All-American image."

"What's wrong with the uncle? What is it with Georgi Zhukov that you're not telling me?"

"Okay, when the old Soviet Union began to come apart in the 1980s, Georgi emigrated to Miami. Unlike a lot of others who came later, Georgi had no criminal record in mother Russia, no telltale jailhouse tats. He got a job as a cab driver, the same as a lot of the other émigrés. However, Georgi was ambitious and soon he got into the wholesale gasoline business."

"What is the wholesale gas business?" Tree asked.

"It's a business where you sell low-grade gas as premium and then pocket the gas taxes. From there, Georgi branched into more favored mob activities, gambling, prostitution, and extortion. For a long time, the local authorities had no interest in Georgi and his Russian Mafia so he was able to fly under the radar for years. By the time the feds woke up to what was happening, Georgi was, well, he was Georgi, pretty much untouchable."

"Do you do business with him?"

Judy mulled the question for a time before carefully choosing her words. "Georgi is not an oligarch and therefore Putin has no real influence over him and that doesn't sit well in Moscow. One has to be careful and say that as far as doing business with him, well, being an honest businesswoman, I have no reason to do business with him now do I?"

"Which is your way of saying you do business with him."

"Take it any way you want," Judy said.

"Would he have kidnapped Becky?"

"With Georgi, you would never say no, but common sense tells me there is no reason for him to be involved in something like that. What would be in it for him besides a shitstorm of unwanted trouble?"

"If I wanted to get hold of Georgi, how would I go about it?" Tree asked.

"That's the point of telling you all this Tree, you don't want to get hold of Georgi. You want to stay as far away from him as you can—if you know what's good for you."

"Supposing I don't know what is good for me," Tree countered. "Can you help me out?"

"Tree, this time I'm serious. Get the hell out of my house."

"At least get in touch with Georgi, tell him I'd like to talk to him. Can you do that for me?"

"Get out!" Judy was yelling. "Get out or I call in the guys who will be only too happy to get you out."

"You wouldn't beat up your beloved former husband, would you?"

"Of course not," Judy said, calming. "I hire people to do that sort of thing for me."

"Tell him, please—"

"Tree!"

He made a hasty departure.

The maid waited outside the library. She did not seem nearly so friendly leading him out as she was when she led him in. Outside, the security guards had taken on a more menacing attitude. The heat of the afternoon sun assailed him as he reached the front gate. Was it his imagination or was he having trouble breathing? He broke into a sweat. The guard at the gate looked as though he never sweated. He inspected Tree much the same way undertakers inspect unpleasant corpses. The gate remained closed. Tree's cellphone sounded.

"I must be out of my mind," Judy said when he answered. "But I'm going to tell you this much…"

"Okay."

"Georgi owns a nightclub in Miami."

"What's it called?"

"Georgi's," Judy answered.

"Tell him I sent you," she added. "That will give him a good laugh just before he slits your throat and drops you into Biscayne Bay."

22

To Tree's surprise—and relief—Gladys was waiting for him in her truck as he came out of the gate onto the street.

"You look as though you've been put through the wringer," Gladys observed when he climbed into the cab.

"It's my I've-just-dealt-with-my-ex-wife look," Tree said.

"Ah, yes, that look," Gladys said.

"Thanks for coming back, Gladys. This is above and beyond the call of duty."

"Hey, it gets me out of the office," Gladys said as she pulled the truck onto Captiva Drive.

"Good," Tree said. "How would you like to spend more time out of the office?"

"Uh oh," Gladys said. "How do I do that?"

"Simply drive me to Miami."

Gladys darted a glance at him. "Are you serious?"

"If you're willing…"

"What's in Miami?"

"A club called Georgi's."

Another darted glance. "You're kidding."

"You know it?"

"Back in the late Eighties when it first opened, Georgi's was hot, a very popular spot. They were lined up to get in. I was Blue Streak back then. They brought in young ladies like myself to entertain the high rollers and Miami in those days was full of high rollers." She gave a rueful smile. "My misspent-but-profitable youth. Some of us grew up and played Carnegie Hall. Some of us never grew up but got to play at Georgi's."

"Did you ever meet the owner, Georgi Zhukov?"

"My God, is that Russian bastard still around?"

"So you do know him?"

"Well, he hired us ladies to perform at his club, perform being a loose description of what he wanted us to do."

"Do you think he'd remember you?"

"I don't know. I was a lot of girls ago. Why would you want to have anything to do with him?"

"His nephew is the Russian cosmonaut, Valentin Baturin."

"What? You think Georgi might have had something to do with Becky's disappearance?"

"You knew him years ago. What do you think?"

"Where a guy like Georgi is concerned, I guess anything is possible. But I'm not sure why he would risk something like an abduction."

"Interesting. Judy said much the same thing."

"Unless for some reason he thought he was helping his nephew," Gladys said.

"Why don't we find out?" Tree said.

"Why don't we do just that?" Gladys was smiling as she hit the gas and the truck leapt ahead.

———

As Gladys headed south on I-75, Tree phoned Freddie. "Where are you?" she promptly demanded.

"I'm with Gladys," Tree said. "We're headed for Miami."

"Becoming an escaped fugitive?"

"Not yet," Tree said.

"I only ask because about an hour ago, the FBI was around here looking for you. An agent with one eye. She is not happy that she can't find you."

"She hasn't called me."

"I'm sure you're going to hear from her. If you're not running from the law, what are you doing going to Miami?"

"I talked to Judy this morning," Tree said.

Freddie's groan came clearly over the line. "Tree, you're supposed to stay away from that woman."

"From what I can gather, Judy feels the same way," Tree said. "But she knows Russians and right now I need help with Russians—which is why we're headed for Miami."

"Don't tell me more," Freddie interrupted. "If I know what you're doing, I have to lie to the FBI, and I don't want to lie to them and get us both into serious trouble."

"I should be back tonight," Tree said.

"I know I've said this a million times—"

"That you love me?"

"I do wonder about that at times like this," Freddie said wearily. "No, what I want to tell you is please, *please* be careful."

"That goes without saying," Tree said.

"No, it doesn't, Tree. No, it does not."

Tree closed his phone and stole a glance at Gladys who was keeping her eyes firmly on the road. "Trouble at home?" she ventured.

"I don't know why it is, but Freddie doesn't seem to like it when the FBI shows up at the door looking for me."

"The true test of a marriage. Can it withstand federal agents pounding on your front door?"

"I feel like shit," Tree said.

"The great thing about not being involved with someone is that I don't have to worry about all the emotional baggage that comes with a relationship."

"What about you and Rex?"

"There is no me and Rex—as I keep trying to tell everyone, even though no one listens, particularly Rex."

"I know Rex tends to complicate things," Tree said.

Gladys shot him another look. "Tree, you complicate things a whole lot more than Rex does. This was supposed to be a nice safe job answering telephones. Instead, here I am driving to Miami in search of Russian gangsters."

"Are you unhappy about that?" Tree asked.

Gladys grinned. "Are you kidding? I wouldn't have it any other way. I always say if your life is boring, start messing with Russian gangsters. Life will suddenly get a whole lot more interesting."

"Well, then, Gladys, your life is about to get a whole lot more interesting."

Gladys grinned.

23

Georgi's may have seen better days but those days were long past. If the club was ever in a fashionable section of Miami it wasn't in one now. In the heat of the late afternoon the place looked forlorn, the color long since bleached out of its walls. The neon Georgi's sign, broken and mounted unsteadily atop the building, looked as though it hadn't worked in years.

Inside, the air was stale with the smell of old beer and lingering cigarette smoke. A bar ran the length of the room. A catwalk thrust out from a low stage into a scattering of round-topped tables, most of which were empty. Two middle-aged women sat at one end of the bar staring up at a big screen TV where black-clad men with automatic weapons were running backwards across a desert. One of the women said, "This goddamn movie doesn't make any sense."

A bartender with muscular forearms bared to show off a skull tattoo turned as Tree and Gladys approached. "Yeah?" His way of greeting the customers, Tree decided.

"Is Georgi around?" Gladys asked.

The bartender's face stayed blank, except for the eyes that darkened with suspicion. "Georgi," he said in accented English as though the name was only vaguely familiar.

"Yeah," Georgi," Gladys said. "His name is on the front of this place."

"What would you want with Georgi?"

"An old friend. I knew him years ago when I worked here."

"You worked here?" The bartender cocked his head a bit, as though he might not be hearing correctly.

"On that stage right over there," Gladys said.

"Olden times," said the bartender. "No one works the stage now."

"Like I said, years ago. You couldn't get in this place."

"No trouble getting in now," said the bartender.

"We were in the neighborhood. I wasn't sure the place was still open."

"Oh, we're open all right," the bartender confirmed.

"I thought I'd drop in, say hello to Georgi. You know, for old time's sake."

"For old time's sake," the bartender repeated as though he had never before heard the expression.

"Is Georgi around? He would remember me as Blue Streak."

"Blue Streak?"

"Is it me?" Gladys asked. "Or do I keep hearing an echo in here?"

The bartender's suspicious eyes shifted to Tree. "Who's your friend?"

"He's my friend."

"A friend," the bartender said.

"There's that echo again," Gladys said. She leaned on the bar, her features hardening. "Listen, friend, is there a problem? I'm here to see Georgi. If he's here, can you let him know that Blue Streak would like to speak to him? If he isn't, we'll leave the echo chamber. How's that?"

The bartender didn't answer immediately, those increasingly suspicious eyes shifting back and forth between Gladys and Tree. "Okay," he said finally.

He drifted away down the bar, disappearing into the gloom. The two women continued to watch the big screen TV mounted above them. "I don't understand any of this shit," one of them said.

"Beats me," said the other.

Gladys and Tree exchanged what-the-hell? looks.

The sound of gunfire reverberated from the screen. Presently, a tall, skinny guy wearing a black suit crossed the stage and jumped down to the floor. He was very pale with large black eyes and black hair shiny with the gel that allowed him to comb it straight back. A carefully trimmed mustache and goatee completed the impression of someone who admired the villains in countless action movies and dressed accordingly.

"What you want?" he demanded. What was pronounced as 'vat.' Maybe he wasn't the result of what happens when you watch too many action movies, Tree reflected. Maybe he was Count Dracula's son, drawn from his coffin by the bartender who had returned to his nonchalant position behind the bar.

Whoever this guy was, he wasn't Georgi.

"What is this?" Gladys was not bothering to hide her irritation. "Who are you?"

"Who I am doesn't matter shit," the skinny guy said. "What matters who you are and what you want."

"Didn't the bartender tell you?"

"Frank didn't tell me shit. Let's move this along. I'm a busy man."

"Yeah, right. I can see that," Gladys said. "Like I told your pal, Frank. I'm an old friend of Georgi's. We dropped by to say hello."

"Yeah, well that won't be possible—to say hello, I mean."

"Why not?"

"Because Georgi's dead."

Gladys looked at him. "Georgi's dead?"

"That's what I just told you, yeah. Dead. Like in not here anymore so you can't visit him."

"When did he die?" Tree asked.

The skinny guy's big eyes spoke multitudes about his dislike for the question. "I dunno," he answered. "A while ago."

"You haven't told us who you are," Gladys said.

"Yeah, well, I'm Nino, Georgi's nephew. I run this place now. What about you? How do you know my uncle?"

"Like I told Frank, back in the Eighties when I was known as Blue Streak, I performed here."

"Is that what they called it? Performing?" Nino was showing a trace of humor.

"That's what Georgi called it, yeah."

Nino broke out a crooked grin that didn't do his face any favors. "Blue Streak, huh? I'll bet you were."

"These days I'm Gladys."

"I like Blue Streak better." The crooked grin stayed in place.

"I'm sorry to hear about Georgi." Gladys's voice dropped to appropriate sadness. "What happened to him?"

"He died."

"Yeah, I got that part," Gladys said. "How long ago?"

"A while ago," answered Nino.

"Is there a cemetery where we might pay our respects?"

"Nah," Nino answered nonchalantly. "We scattered him to the four winds. Earth to earth, and all that shit."

"Hey, Nino, what the hell?"

Tree turned to see a trio of men the size of refrigerators lumbering into the club. They were dressed in identical blue track suits.

Nino looked suddenly a whole lot more nervous and a whole lot less nonchalant. "Hey, guys. How did it go?"

"Deed's done boss man, no worries," reported the smallest of the three, although small was hardly the word you ordinarily would use to describe him. He spoke in a gruff tone similar to the other gruff tones Tree had heard since entering Georgi's.

"Yeah, glad to hear it," Nino said to the men. "I'll be right with you. Just finishing up with a couple of customers."

"Customers?" The three refrigerators chuckled in unison.

"Okay, folks, I've told you what I know. We're finished here." Nino's accompanying scowl said he wanted the two of them out.

"Sorry about Georgi," Gladys said.

"Yeah, a real tragedy." Nino didn't sound as though it was a tragedy at all.

"We appreciate your time," Tree said, taking Gladys by the arm and turning her toward the door.

As she passed, Gladys eyed the refrigerators speculatively. "Love those track suits," she breathed.

She received a trio of glares in response.

———————

The scorching heat of the Florida sun drained the color from the bleak landscape outside Georgi's. Gladys fished a pair of sunglasses out of her jacket pocket as they crossed the street to where she had parked the truck.

"That was a waste of time," Tree said as they got into the hot cab.

"You think so?" Gladys said as she started the engine and the AC roared through the interior.

"You don't?"

"Hey, you're the private detective. I just answer the phones."

"Gladys," Tree said impatiently. "Tell me what you're thinking."

"I'm thinking that if Nino back there told me the world is round, I would start to have second thoughts."

"Georgi isn't dead? He's still alive?"

"Maybe he's dead. Maybe he's not. Maybe Nino is up to something. Maybe he's not."

"Okay. What are you suggesting?"

"I'm suggesting that we're in no hurry. Why don't we sit here for a while in my lovely new truck, enjoying the AC and the lovely scenery—and see what happens?"

Which they did, keeping an eye on the club across the street. The amazing thing to Tree was that even as it grew late in the afternoon, as the skies began to darken and the warm languid breeze sharpened into a hot wind, no one came to Georgi's. As he watched, Tree's eyes began to flutter and close, and he remembered why he so hated the private detective's stock in trade, the stakeout. Sitting still hour after hour always had the effect of putting him to sleep. That was why, he had long since decided, he was never going to be a good detective. He could not stay awake.

A blast of hot wind shook the truck and awakened Tree with a jerk. In front of him, a garbage bin went spinning past. Another wind gust jerked at the truck.

"Getting mean out there," Gladys observed.

Tree rubbed at his eyes. "Was I asleep?"

"You were," Gladys said. "But you woke up just in time, Sleeping Beauty." She nodded in the direction of the windshield. "We've got movement."

Sure enough, the three track-suited refrigerators had stepped outside, fighting against the wind. They stood at the curb, big fellows looking miserable, having trouble maintaining their balance. Presently, a Ford SUV turned the corner with Nino at the wheel. Two of the refrigerators got in the back while the third slid in beside Nino. As soon as the three were settled, Nino sped off along the street.

Gladys looked at Tree.

"What the hell," he said. "We might as well."

Gladys was all smiles as she started along the street after the Ford SUV.

24

B y the time Nino in his Ford SUV drove into what Tree
was pretty sure was the neighborhood adjacent to Miami
known as Allapattah, the heavy black sky gave up and poured
hard rain onto the district, accompanied by a whipping wind
of hurricane proportions. If the world was about to end, Tree
reflected as Gladys fought to keep her truck on the road, then
this might well be the beginning of that end. He would die in
Allapattah, he thought.

Another wind blast shook the truck, Gladys gripped the
wheel with white knuckles. "Did you see where they turned?"

Tree pulled himself out of his reverie as they passed an intersection and he caught a glimpse of the Ford's disappearing
taillights. "Make a right," he said to Gladys.

"Jesus," she said, twisting the wheel hard to execute a sharp,
skidding turn. Day had become night as Gladys drove beneath
an overpass onto a broad thoroughfare flanked by warehouses.
At a stoplight, the Ford made another right onto NW Seventh
Avenue, passing a brightly lit parking garage and then turning
into the darkness of a side street, slowing as it reached a low-
slung adobe structure on the left. The Ford turned into the
drive beside the structure.

A vacant lot next door was fronted by a chain-link fence.
Gladys swung through an opening in the fence, switching off
the headlights as she brought the truck to a stop so that she
faced the Ford fifty yards or so away. Through the rain it was
hard to see for certain but it appeared as though Nino and his
refrigerators had already exited the SUV and entered what now
looked to Tree like a boarded-up garage.

Gladys said, "Reach into the glove compartment for me, will you Tree?"

Tree leaned forward and popped the lid to reveal the Glock automatic lying atop the owner's manual. "Hand me the gun," Gladys said.

He looked over at her. "Do you think we need this?"

"Check the private dick's user guide. When operating in strange, dark neighborhoods with a garage full of Russian gangsters, always make sure you come armed."

Tree handed her the gun.

"Thanks," she said, sticking the Glock into the belt of her jeans and then opening the driver's-side door and starting out.

Tree was about to offer further, well-reasoned objections but it was too late. Gladys was outside. Tree fought against the wind to get his door open. As soon as he squeezed out, he was nearly blown off the ground. He could see Gladys, already soaked to the skin, hanging onto the hood of her truck for support. Across the way, a piece of flying metal debris slammed into the side of the Ford. From somewhere nearby came the sound of breaking glass barely heard over the shriek of the wind.

A door in the side of the garage popped open and Nino lurched out, leaning hard into the wind and the slanting rain, followed shortly by the refrigerators wrestling a heavyset, black-bearded man with shoulder-length black hair whipped around in the wind. His chest and hands were wrapped in red duct tape. Gladys jabbed frantically as Tree moved closer. "What?" he yelled.

"Georgi," she yelled. "That's Georgi!"

As Tree took in the man being manhandled toward Nino's Ford, a piece of metal came spinning out of the darkness, slamming into one of the refrigerators. Tree could hear his cry over the freight-train sound the wind was making. The others were thrown into disarray, allowing Georgi to break free and stagger away. Gladys, Glock in hand, immediately charged forward. One of the refrigerators pivoted awkwardly to face her. She raised the gun and for an instant Tree thought for sure Gladys would shoot the guy. But the refrigerator ducked away, retreating back so that Georgi could blunder past Gladys and fall into Tree's waiting arms. Georgi's broad Slavic face was wet and full of confusion. "Who are you?" he managed to ask.

"People who can help," was all Tree could think to say as he propelled Georgi toward the truck.

"That is good," Georgi said. "Because otherwise, those bastards will kill me."

"Get in the truck," Tree said.

Georgi nodded and Tree maneuvered him to the passenger side, managed to force the door open so that Georgi could crawl in the back. Once that was done, Tree made his way around the truck, got the door open and managed to struggle behind the wheel. He started the engine and threw the truck into gear as Gladys flashed in front of him, followed by one of the refrigerators. Tree hit the gas pedal. The truck lurched forward, clipping the refrigerator, sending him flying away into the darkness. Tree slammed to a stop and instantly the passenger door opened and Gladys, panting hard, jumped inside, yelling, "Go! Get the hell out of here."

Swinging the truck onto the drive beside the garage, Tree followed it onto NW Seventh Avenue.

He feared the Ford's headlights flashing in the rearview mirror, the indication that Nino and his pals were coming after them. But to his relief there was only rainy darkness.

Gladys turned around to Georgi slumped in the back, looking like a bedraggled mummy swathed in red tape. "How are you doing, Georgi?"

"Can you get me out of this tape?" Georgi asked in a thick, gravelly accent Tree imagined was required before you could become a bearded, overweight Russian gangster.

Tree glanced into the rearview mirror. Georgi's black eyes had lit with surprise. "My God, Blue," he said, "is that you? Blue Streak?"

"It's been a long time Georgi," Gladys said. "I'm surprised you remember me."

"Remember you? My little fox, how could I ever forget you? Impossible! And now, like a miracle from heaven, you show up in a hurricane to save my ass. How is this even imaginable?"

"They told us you were dead," Gladys said.

"That bastard Nino, the goddamn nephew who betrayed me to my enemies, he certainly wants me dead. You go to the club? Is that it?"

"That's where we ran into Nino," Gladys said. "The next time you're talking to him, you should let him know he's a lousy liar."

"He's a stupid ass, but you must have scared him, my little fox. Those bastards were moving me to who-knows-where when you came along." Georgi grinned as he nodded to the back of Tree's head. "Who is you friend? Who is this old guy?"

"This is Tree Callister," Gladys explained. "Tree's a private detective on Sanibel Island. I answer the phones in his office."

Georgi let out a burst of laughter. "You, little fox? You answer phones? The famous Blue Streak *answers phones?*"

"Georgi, I'm known as Gladys now. Gladys Demchuk. That's my real name. Blue Streak has been retired."

Georgi arranged his massive face into a look of infinite sadness. "This is so unfortunate. A calamity. Your talents were infinite. But you know…Gladys? Gladys. Now that fate or God or whatever has brought us together again, perhaps it is time for you to free me from this terrible tape. What do you think, little fox?"

"Not so fast there, comrade," Gladys said. "Maybe we'll wait a bit longer before we do that, get ourselves out of Miami, and then decide on the best course of action."

"My little fox—Gladys." Georgi's voice was coated with innocence. "You save my life and you don't trust me?"

"We save your life *and* we don't trust you," Gladys confirmed.

"Give me a break, please," Georgi said. "I am wet through and through. My muscles ache from being tied up. I cannot even scratch my nose. I am not much threat to you. After all, you rescued me and you have the gun, not me."

"Why was Nino holding you?" Tree called from the front.

"Nino is a son of a bitch, that's what Nino is. He thinks I am old and finished and he can take over everything. Now he will have another thing coming, and what is coming will not be pleasant, believe me." In the darkness, Georgi's smile filled his face. "I must tell you, though, it will be impossible for him to have another thing coming until you free me."

"Yeah, well, while you're plotting revenge, Georgi, the question Tree and myself have to deal with is what we do with you once we do untie you," Gladys said.

"This is an excellent question, my little fox," Georgi said agreeably. "Because of what happened tonight, Nino will not let it stand. While I will eventually extract revenge for his betrayal, it is unfortunate that for the moment, Nino is out there in the darkness, angry, and very dangerous. Unfortunately for you he will soon figure out who you are and come after you."

"What about you, Georgi? Won't he be coming after you, too?"

"Yes, naturally," Georgi said. "But the difference is, this

time I will be prepared for him. Nino knows that so he will be very cautious. That is why, my two friends, you will soon discover that whether you like it or not, you need me. I'm afraid that although you have me tied up, you are now also tied to me. You both will need me for protection—that is if you wish to go on living."

25

As they neared Fort Myers, the rain let up so that it was no longer an opaque wall in the headlights; the wind wasn't the same roaring freight train as before, reduced to a shrieking opera singer; and the realization grew that they had a notorious Russian gangster tied up in the backseat that they had no idea what to do with.

Georgi appeared unconcerned, having fallen asleep.

"We can't take him to my place," opined Gladys. "Nino knows who I am. As soon as he's able to find out where I live, he'll come looking for his uncle." She stole a quick look at Tree. "However, they don't know you, Tree, and they have no idea where you live."

Tree thought of Freddie and how she might react. Not well, he immediately concluded. Not well at all.

From the back, Georgi stirred and said, "My friends, my fate is in your hands. Of course, you could release me, but then where would I go? I would become the duck sitting for those bastards."

"What about your nephew?" Tree asked.

"My nephew?" Georgi sounded confused. "What nephew you are talking about? Surely not the nephew who would put a bullet in my head."

"Another nephew. Valentin. The cosmonaut."

Georgi made a dismissive sound. "That asshole? The last thing he would wish is me at his door, believe me."

"What is it with you, Georgi?" Gladys asked. "Are all your nephews assholes?"

"Pretty much, that is the case, I'm afraid."

"Where is Valentin now?" Gladys asked.

"Who knows? Flying around in space. Who gives a shit? Why are you interested in him, anyway?"

"You haven't heard?"

"Heard what?"

"Becky McPhee has been abducted," Tree said.

"Who is Becky McPhee?" Georgi sounded more confused than ever.

"You must have heard about her. She is the astronaut who says the world is coming to an end."

"My world has been coming to an end for some time now, maybe that is why I do not know this Becky," Georgi said. "I have no time to worry about anyone else's world."

"We understand that Becky is involved with Valentin."

"I know nothing about this. When you are being held for weeks in a locked room by murderous bastards, you do not receive much information."

"Then you wouldn't have kidnapped anybody, would you Georgi?" Tree asked.

Georgi issued another burst of laughter. "My friend, people are busy kidnapping *me*, they give me no time to do kidnapping on my own. And in a million years I cannot imagine I would kidnap my idiot nephew's girlfriend who says it is the end of the world and who I do not know."

"What about Valentin?" Gladys asked. "Would he be capable of something like that?"

The coins began to drop from Georgi's eyes. "Is this what it is all about? You think I kidnapped Valentin's woman? Is that why you came for me? My God. I must tell you, I appreciate what you did, no matter what the circumstances, but honestly, I have fallen into the hands of a couple of fools."

Tree gritted his teeth as he turned onto the Daniels Parkway. "You haven't answered the question," he said.

"Excuse me, I have been distracted by madness and have forgotten what you asked."

Gladys reframed the question: "Could Valentin have kidnapped Becky McPhee?"

That drew a derisive snort from Georgi. "Valentin is capable of doing what his masters tell him and that includes flying around in a tin can. Otherwise, he is useless for anything."

———

To her credit, Freddie performed admirably trying not to look stunned when presented with a rain-soaked Gladys and Tree, accompanied by a burly guy, equally rain-soaked, wrapped more or less in red duct tape, whose presence seemed to fill the room.

Once Gladys had freed him from the encumbering red duct tape, Georgi quickly moved in his own melodramatic way to smooth things over—at least as much as they could be smoothed, which, judging from the look on Freddie's face, was pretty much impossible.

"You must be the most beautiful wife of the man who today saved my life," he said, throwing out his recently-freed arms in joyous embrace. "You must tell me your name, my little fox."

"Who are you?" Freddie demanded.

"Me?" Georgi appeared supremely pleased by Freddie's question. "Why I am a terrible, awful, Russian gangster, unworthy to draw the next breath, but nonetheless saved from dreadful assassins by your beautiful husband and my dear, good friend, the famous Miss Blue Streak—"

"Uh, like I told you before, Georgi, I'm Gladys now."

"Ah, but you will always be Blue to me, my little fox. None-theless—" and here he gave an expansive shrug—"I will obey your every wish. Gladys, it shall be!"

Tree stepped into the fray, announcing, "Freddie this is Georgi Zhukov. Georgi, as you have already guessed, this is my wife, Freddie—Fredryka."

At that Georgi threw out his arms again as if attempting to embrace the world. "Such an immense pleasure, Fredryka. It is my honor to meet the wife of this man—the hero of my life, the savior of my life!"

"You keep saying that," Freddie said dryly.

"It is true!" proclaimed Georgi.

"I think Gladys may have played a role when it comes to lifesaving," Tree put in.

Georgi seemed not to hear him. "Now your wonderful husband allows me to hide out in your beautiful home—"

"He does?" Freddie shot Tree what could only be termed a stink-eyed look.

"Otherwise," Georgi rambled on, "I will be outside on these mean Florida streets tonight, unarmed and unprotected, and on those streets I most certainly would die."

"I'm sorry about this, Freddie," Gladys interjected. "Georgi really is in danger and right now there is nowhere else to take him."

"I know this is a silly suggestion—it must be a silly suggestion because I've offered it so many times over the years and no one has taken me up on it yet."

"How could any suggestion you make be silly, my little fox?" proclaimed Georgi. "What is your suggestion? I am all ears."

"My suggestion is that if you're in trouble, you go to the police," Freddie said.

"The police?" Georgi sounded genuinely shocked by the idea. "I cannot go to the police."

"No? Why not?" demanded Freddie.

"Because in their eyes I am the bad guy. I go to them, I tell them my nephew is trying to kill me, you know what they will say?"

"What?" Freddie asked.

"Good! That's what they will say. One less stinking Russian to deal with. No, if I stand any chance of surviving it is with my good friends, your husband and this beautiful woman, Blue Streak, who was once the love of my life."

Tree turned to Gladys in surprise. "He was?"

"It's Gladys," Gladys said impatiently. "I'm not Blue Streak."

"And you, Mrs. Freddie, you truly are a goddess," enthused Georgi.

"A weak goddess," Freddie sighed. "Susceptible to the whims of her crazy husband."

Georgi laughed and said, "Please, a beautiful woman such as yourself, I cannot believe you are subject to the whims of any man. And please, you must call me Georgi."

———————

Freed from his duct tape bonds and mostly dried out, Georgi stated that he had not eaten for days. He proceeded to devour a leftover chicken pot pie. He consumed the salmon pasta dish Freddie had prepared, naïve enough to expect Tree home for dinner. The pasta was followed by three ham, lettuce, and tomato sandwiches, washed down with three quarters of a bottle of red wine. For dessert, Freddie made the mistake of offering him a scoop of Häagen-Dazs dulce de leche. The entire container soon disappeared.

After he had almost literally eaten them out of house and home, Georgi announced that he was dead tired. Freddie set him up in the guest room while Tree scrounged up a robe that more or less fit Georgi's massive frame. The Russian was snoring loudly by the time Tree turned off the bedroom light and shut the door behind him.

He found Freddie curled on an armchair in the living room, sipping a glass of water. Gladys was sprawled on a sofa, half asleep. "Gladys has filled me in on what you two idiots have been up to," Freddie said in a resigned voice. "Let me see, over the years we've ended up housing a twelve-year-old kid, a dog, an ex-wife or two, your brother—"

"Half-brother," corrected Tree. "And he never stayed the night."

"And now, to cap it all off, a Russian gangster who, from what I can understand from Gladys, is being hunted by other Russian gangsters."

"Yup, that about sums it up," Gladys agreed. She yawned and then struggled to her feet. "I'm going to call it a night. I've got to be up bright and early for my day job—answering telephones."

"Who knows, Gladys," Freddie said ruefully. "If you stick around long enough, you may actually get to answer a phone."

"I look forward to that day," Gladys said. "But I am not holding my breath."

"Listen, Gladys, thanks for this," Tree said.

"All in a day's work," said Gladys with a sigh. "Although, I'm not sure what we accomplished other than to free a Russian leopard from his cage. Given what I remember of Georgi from the old days, I'm not so sure he isn't more dangerous than his nephew, Nino."

"You know, she is probably right," Freddie said, after Gladys had departed. "What did you accomplish today other than ending up with an oversized house guest who's almost certain to get you into more trouble than you were in before—me too, for that matter?"

"I don't seem to be doing much of anything that helps," Tree conceded. "I started out with the thought I was helping protect Becky McPhee. Instead, I seem to have enabled her abduction. And then, setting out to find her, I've ended up nursemaid to a Russian hood, who says he doesn't know anything about his nephew Valentin or Becky McPhee."

"That's what he *says*," Freddie added.

"You don't believe him?"

"Tree, the words Russian and gangster aren't ordinarily used in conjunction with the phrase, 'telling the truth.'"

"I suppose you could be right," Tree conceded.

"Who knows what this guy has been up to? He seems amiable enough, but do you think in a million years you can trust him?"

Tree sat there trying to imagine how he might be able to trust a Russian gangster held prisoner by his own nephew. His cellphone started making sounds. When he opened it up a voice said, "There's been a terrible storm here."

"Who is this?"

"A lot of damage as far as I can see, but the house is all right. At least, I think it's all right."

Tree was suddenly struck by a cold realization. "Becky? Becky McPhee? Is that you?"

"I didn't know who else to call," she said in a lost voice.

"Becky, are you all right?"

"Like I said, the storm," she answered, her voice breaking. "I need help. Can you come? Please? Something terrible has happened."

26

The rain had redoubled its assault along the coastline, a world of water and darkness out the windshield of Freddie's Mercedes. She drove with grim determination while Tree sat beside her wondering what the hell they were headed into.

There had been tense debate between them over what to do about the sleeping Georgi. "He's sound asleep, he'll be fine," Tree had argued.

"I don't like the idea of being alone with a Russian gangster," Freddie had countered. "I'm coming with you."

"You should stay here in case he decides to steal the furniture."

"You said it yourself. He's sound asleep," Freddie had said. "He's not going to steal the furniture."

"Don't be too sure about that," Tree said

"Besides, I don't want you going alone. You need me with you."

"Why do I need you?"

"Because if I'm being honest about it, whatever happens you will need someone else to be present to back up the story you tell the police they otherwise won't believe."

"This could be dangerous," Tree had argued.

"What is it you always say? Danger is my middle name?"

"I never say that."

"Yes, you do."

"If that's the case, danger is *my* middle name, it's not yours."

"I'm coming with you," Freddie had said, "and that's the end of it."

And it was.

The heavy rain had reduced itself to a light shower by the time they saw the telltale gleam of light originating from a wood-frame cabin outside Everglades City.

The ramshackle cabin sat atop stilts, faded and weather-beaten, all but defeated by the hammering nature had delivered over the years. Everything along the Gulf coast is in a continual fight for survival, someone had once observed to Tree. This cabin was on the verge of finally losing that fight. Overhead, storm clouds blocked the moon and turned the water beyond the house black. If there was any doubt that Freddie and Tree had found the right place, Becky sat on the front steps to welcome them.

She was naked and she was holding a gun.

The gun was loosely held in her hand. Her eyes were focused somewhere far away. She didn't appear to notice them for a time despite Freddie calling, "Becky? Are you okay? Becky?"

When she finally acknowledged their presence, it was with a crooked smile. "I...didn't do it..."

Freddie leaned slowly forward to ease the gun from Becky's hand. "You probably don't need this," she said quietly. Holding the gun, she glanced back at Tree. "I'm going to get a blanket out of the car for Becky. Why don't you go ahead and check inside?"

Tree nodded and went up the steps. As he reached the deck, the clouds cleared enough so that moonlight illuminated a becalmed sea and the pilings below the house where a dock should have been. A screen door was wide open. Tree stepped into a living room paneled with rough planks, a big brick and tin fireplace over which was mounted the marlin that the State of Florida had mandated for all cabins with fireplaces. A Norman

Rockwell print of a grandfatherly type helping a tow-haired lad land a big fish was on another wall beside ancient mariners' maps. Tired old furniture was visible through the gloom.

Tree moved across the dark hardwood floor into a kitchenette. It had been a long time since anyone had used it. A short corridor led to a bedroom. The door was open allowing light from the other room to spill across a double brass bed and the body of a man lying facedown.

Closer to the bed, Tree could see that the man was young and naked. It looked as though he had been shot in the side of the head. The bedclothes on which he lay were soaked in blood. Tree leaned over the body and felt for a pulse. As he expected, there was none. He straightened and looked around, trying not to think about the complications of him discovering yet another dead body, in particular, a body watched over by a world-famous astronaut, naked and holding the gun she may have used to shoot the young man. The naked astronaut, incidentally, who had recently disappeared after going off with Tree; the naked astronaut with whom in some quarters he was suspected of being in collusion. Tree finding a dead body would do nothing to allay those suspicions. The exact opposite, in fact.

Shit!

A heap of what looked like Becky's clothes lay on a wicker chair in the corner. The man's clothes were in a careless wad on the floor at the side of the bed. Tree scooped Becky's clothes off the chair and then backed carefully out of the bedroom. At the threshold, he stopped and used Becky's panties to polish the door latch. He crossed the living room and did the same to the entrance door latch.

A mist had replaced the rain and now clung to the deck. A few scuttling clouds partially obscured the moon. Tree went down the stairs. Freddie was at the Mercedes, Becky seated on the passenger side with the door open, trembling, wrapped in a blanket. Tree handed her the clothes. "You can get dressed," he said. Becky nodded slightly. Her eyes, he noticed, remained far, far away.

"Who is that in the cabin?" he asked.

It was as though the question took a long time to reach her ears. When it did, her eyes briefly lit and she said, "I'd like to get dressed."

Tree glanced around, seeing the outlines of an SUV at the side of the house. "Whose car is that?"

"He brought me here," she answered.

"From where?"

She fell silent. Freddie placed a reassuring hand on Becky's blanketed shoulder. "It's all right, you don't have to say anything more until the police get here."

At that, Becky's eyes widened in alarm. "You haven't called the police?"

"Not yet," Freddie said.

"No! Not the police." She looked desperately up at Tree. "That's why I called you, Callister. You're the only person I can trust. If the police come, oh God..." she trailed off. There were tears in her eyes.

"You told us you didn't do it," Tree said.

"No."

"Tell us what happened," Tree said.

She swallowed hard. "Please...let me get dressed."

Tree and Freddie exchanged quick glances. Freddie offered Becky a warm smile. "Why don't you do that? We'll leave you alone for a few minutes."

Becky nodded and lifted her legs inside so that Freddie could shut the passenger door. Freddie drew Tree away. "You found someone in the cabin?" she asked.

"A dead man in the bedroom."

Freddie grimaced. "We have to call the police," she said. "We can't just walk away from this. A body upstairs. She's sitting out here with a gun."

Tree considered the endless complications that would ensue as soon as the authorities became involved. Not to mention the ravenous press mob that would descend. He was about to agree with Freddie that as much as he hated to do it, there was no real choice.

Then they both heard the sound of an engine turning over.

They turned in time to see the Mercedes start forward. Becky was behind the wheel. Before they could react, she stepped on the gas. The Mercedes shot down the roadway and disappeared into the mist.

27

I don't believe that just happened," Tree said.
"You left the key fob in the car," Freddie said.

"I did," admitted Tree.

"I've told you many times not to do that."

"Yes, you have," Tree conceded.

"Then take it from me, it did happen. Becky drove off in our car. Now what?"

Yes, damned good question. Now what indeed? Tree pondered. When it came to the most unexpected turns of events in the life of Tree Callister—and there were many from which to choose—this one was right at the top. Only the truly amazing fact that given his stupidity, he had managed to survive this long, was higher.

"Because here is the thing," Freddie went on. "We are standing here in the middle of the night. There is a dead man lying in the cabin over there. I am holding the gun that probably killed him. My fingerprints are on the gun. Meantime, when you were in the cabin, I'll bet you took time to erase any prints belonging to Becky. Maybe at some point Becky's DNA will show up in whatever fluids she and her partner might have exchanged and left on the bed. For now, thanks to you, there is probably no sign that she was ever here. But there is lots of evidence that we are here because, well, here we are."

"Give me the gun," Tree said.

She handed it to him. "What are you going to do with it?"

He didn't answer but turned and started away. "Tree," she called to him as he faded into the mist. She hurried after him and found him at the shore crouched against the wind. Before she could even think about trying to stop him, he heaved the gun as far as he could into the churning water.

Freddie had to shout over the wind. "You shouldn't have done that!"

"I know," Tree said. "But I did it. They may find it at some point but not tonight."

"God, Tree," Freddie said in exasperation. "What are you doing?"

"She said she didn't do it."

"You believe her?"

"Right now we don't have a lot of choice."

Tree moved away from the shore and got on his cellphone. "Hello, Gladys. It's me."

"Tree? What the hell? What time is it?"

"It's late," he said. "Listen, I'm out in Everglades City—"

"What?"

"Outside Everglades City, actually."

"What the hell are you doing there?"

"It's a long story but as usual it ends with me in trouble and stranded with no car."

"Jumping Jesus," Gladys said.

"I'm with Freddie," Tree said. "Look, I'm sorry about this, but I need you to come out here and pick us up and do it as quick as you can."

"Yeah, okay," Gladys said. She sounded wide awake now.

"There's one more thing," Tree added.

"What's that?"

"Will you stop at our place and pick up Georgi?"

"You sure you want Georgi mixed up in this?"

"Yes," Tree said. "And one more thing."

"Yes?"

"Bring your gun."

28

Headlights flashed through the mist and Gladys's truck drove into view.

As soon as she brought the vehicle to a stop, the passenger door popped open and Georgi lumbered out, looking sleep-deprived and more disheveled than ever. He also looked unhappy. "What is this?" he demanded. "What have you got me into? Why am I here?"

Gladys came out of the truck, squeezing into blue Latex gloves. A woman prepared for a crime scene. "Have you called the police?" She addressed Tree.

Tree shook his head. Freddie said, "He wouldn't—as usual."

"Thank God for that," said Georgi. "I cannot be here if there are police."

"None of us can," Tree said. He said to Gladys, "Did you bring more gloves?"

"A box of them in the truck."

"Would you get them, please."

Once everyone had struggled into gloves, Tree said, "Come with me, Georgi, I want to show you something."

"What? What you want to show me?" Georgi's face filled with an expression of crafty suspicion, trying to figure the angles, concerned about how those angles might affect him.

"Just come with me," Tree said.

Georgi followed Tree up the steps and into the living room. He came to a stop. "I do not like this, Tree. What are you doing?"

"Follow me."

He trailed Tree into the bedroom. Georgi didn't show much reaction when he saw the body on the bed. Tree said, "Tell me who that is."

Georgi was moving around the bed to get a closer look at the body. "This person means nothing to me. Why should he?"

"Do you know who he is?"

"His name is Yuri Revin. I believe he is a cosmonaut. A close friend of my good-for-nothing nephew, Valentin."

"Someone who knew what they were doing came in here and shot him."

Georgi actually looked surprised. "What are you getting at? You cannot believe I shot this Yuri who means nothing to me."

"Georgi, you're a gangster. This is the sort of thing gangsters do."

"I am a gangster, yes, but I am a gangster who lately has been kidnapped and held against my will. I have not been in a position to kill anyone. Also, I happen to be a gangster who kills people I know. I had nothing to do with killing someone I don't know."

"What about Nino? Would he do this?"

"Nino, definitely. He would shoot you. He would certainly shoot me. But why he would shoot Yuri Revin? I don't know, but I highly doubt it."

A rich-brown leather wallet lay on the dresser beside the kind of expensive watch Tree would expect a cosmonaut to wear, an Omega Speedmaster. A money clip could barely contain the fifty and one-hundred-dollar bills. Tree gingerly picked up the wallet, calfskin, from Montblanc. It contained gold credit cards, a Florida driver's license assigned to Yuri Vladimirovich Revin, and three photographs. Two of the photos showed a nude woman. In the third photo, a selfie, Yuri hugged against the same woman, the two of them grinning happily.

Tree would have expected the woman to be Becky McPhee. But it wasn't.

The woman was Becky's sister, Miranda.

"There's your answer my friend," stated Georgi, looking over Tree's shoulder at the photos. "The woman with Yuri tonight found those photos. Her lover with another lover. She then shot her betraying lover. A crime of passion. A very old crime indeed."

Tree didn't like the idea, and Freddie certainly didn't, however, there was little choice but to bring Georgi back to Andy Rosse Lane. A miserable Georgi at that, unhappy at being hauled out of bed in the middle of the night. As soon as Gladys dropped them off, Georgi, grumbling, retreated to the guest bedroom.

Exhausted himself, Tree fell into bed beside Freddie who immediately rose up on an elbow and asked, "What are you going to do?"

The question Tree hated most in his life, principally because he seldom had a ready answer. That was never truer than it was tonight.

"What do we do about the car?" Freddie went on. "Do we report it stolen? More to the point, what do we do *without* a car?"

"I can barely keep my eyes open let alone think," Tree ventured.

"We've also got to somehow deal with the fact that we not only walked away from a murder scene after allowing the number-one suspect to get away, but we also worked hard to cover up the fact we were even *at* the murder scene."

"Yes," agreed Tree, fighting to stay awake.

"I thought Becky was with Valentin Baturin. What was she doing with his friend, Yuri Revin?"

"Yuri and Becky were on the space station together," Tree said.

"Okay, space station lovers," Freddie said. "Now there's a story for you. But then you find photos of Yuri with Becky's sister, Miranda."

"Georgi thinks Becky found the photos and shot Yuri. A crime of passion."

"That makes as much sense as anything," Freddie said. "Is that what you believe happened?"

"I don't know," Tree said.

"Then there is the problem of the Russian gangster asleep in our guest bedroom."

"Yes, there is," Tree agreed.

"Tree, we are in a lot of shit," Freddie concluded.

Tree had begun to snore softly.

29

SIX DAYS BEFORE THE END OF THE WORLD

Exhausted, Tree slept a deep sleep undisturbed by his usual fervid dreams. When he awoke, it was nearly ten o'clock and Freddie, looking amazingly fresh and rested, was standing at the bottom of the bed holding a cup of coffee.

"Don't think for a moment this coffee is for you," she said.

"Never crossed my mind," said Tree, struggling to sit up.

"If you can manage to lift your carcass out of bed, there is coffee in the kitchen."

"Much appreciated," Tree said, trying to shake loose the cobwebs that clung stubbornly to the inner recesses of his head.

"Also, as though by magic, two of your problems have been more or less solved."

"Good," Tree said. "Which problems?"

"The Mercedes is in the driveway."

"You're kidding. It's back?"

"It was there when I got up this morning. Also, Georgi."

"Oh, God, Georgi," Tree groaned. "What's he done now?"

"He's left."

"Gone?"

"Gone."

"Gone where?"

"I haven't the faintest idea. The Mercedes is back. Georgi is gone. That's the sum total of what I know."

"I wonder how the Mercedes got here."

"However, if you're looking for evidence in your life that

just before it rains again the sun comes out, there is a third problem which you might have anticipated but probably didn't."

"What's that?"

"The Federal Bureau of Investigation."

"The FBI. What about the FBI?"

"There's a one-eyed FBI agent…"

"I can't do this," Tree said agitatedly. "I don't want to deal with her today."

"Too bad. She's waiting for you in the living room."

Drew Castle didn't stand as Tree, hastily dressed in T-shirt and cargo shorts, staggered into the living room. Instead, Drew sat forward on the sofa, hands dangling between her legs, studying Tree with that one good eye, perhaps trying to ascertain whether she was confronting an international terrorist or a bumbling fool.

She sat back, her body relaxing, seeming to have chosen the bumbling fool.

"You look all tuckered out, Mr. Callister," she observed. "Late night?"

"You know how it is," Tree said. "The life of a private detective."

"Wild and crazy, huh?"

Freddie lingered behind Tree saying nothing. Tree said, "What can I do for you Agent Castle?"

"Well, you know, Tree, we've been trying to get hold of you."

"Have you now?"

"You know damned well we have."

"But my esteemed lawyer, T. Emmett Hawkins, doesn't like it when I talk to law enforcement when he's not present."

"An innocent man shouldn't have to worry about talking to law enforcement," Drew said.

"An innocent man listens to his lawyer," Tree countered. "That's how he stays innocent."

"Would you like to speak to your lawyer now?" Drew asked.

"Do I need to speak to my lawyer?"

Drew allowed a smile. "I wouldn't think so. But let's see how it goes. If at some point you feel the need, we will stop and you can call Mr. Hawkins."

"That sounds fair enough," Tree said.

"Tree, if you've been paying any attention to the television or radio or the newspapers, taken note of the number of press people camped out on Sanibel and Captiva, you will probably understand that the search for and the investigation of the mystery surrounding Becky McPhee continues, fueled by Ms. McPhee's assertion that the end of the world is coming in—what?—how many days?"

"I'm trying not to pay attention."

"Well, much of the world is paying very close attention, which puts a great deal of pressure on us to find Becky."

"Understandable," Tree agreed. "Although if we're all soon going to die, maybe it's a waste of time."

"Try telling that to my bosses in Miami," Drew said.

"They don't believe the world will come to an end?"

"They believe I should find Becky. Which brings me back to your involvement in this, and the disturbing fact that at every turn in our ongoing inquiry, your name seems to come up."

"I don't see how that's possible."

"For example, I previously asked you about a man named Valentin Baturin. Mr. Baturin seems to have disappeared. In our attempts to locate him, his association with a woman named Judith Markov has come to light. Mrs. Markov it turns out is the widow of a notorious Russian oligarch named Alexei Markov. He died a few years ago and now Mrs. Markov has taken over his business interests, running them from here in South Florida. Much to everyone's surprise, Mrs. Markov has become something of a feared presence in international business circles, a ruthless, cutthroat businesswoman willing to do whatever it takes to attain her ends.

"Further, and again, much to our surprise, we discovered that before she married Alexei Markov, Judith was known as Judy and was married to you."

"What has my long-ago marriage to Judy got to do with anything?"

Drew ignored Tree's question and continued: "At the same time, as we began digging into Valentin Baturin's background, guess what else we found? We discovered that Valentin's uncle is a well-known Russian gangster located in Miami named Georgi Zhukov. It turns out that not only has the Miami office of the Bureau been investigating Mr. Zhukov's various activities including money laundering, prostitution, and scams involving fraudulent Medicare payments, but he too has gone missing."

"I'm getting confused by all this," Tree interjected.

Again, Drew ignored him. "Nonetheless, our agents, diligent men and women that they are, continued to watch a downtown club, Georgi's, which, as you might suspect, is owned by Mr. Zhukov and where he is said to hang out. While they are watching the place, who should turn up but a man and a woman who entered the club. The surveillance photos the agents took are disappointingly blurry given the modern technology available, but the man in the pictures looks an awful lot like you, Tree."

"That's right," Tree said.

Before she could stop herself, Drew looked taken aback. "You were at Georgi's?"

"I was," Tree said.

"What were you doing in Miami at Georgi's?"

"I was there to find Georgi." Tree made it sound as though the search for Georgi was entirely reasonable.

"And why would you be looking for him?"

"You explained it yourself—he's Valentin's uncle. I thought he might know something about Valentin and therefore help me find Becky."

"Why would you be looking for Becky?"

"Because you and the local police seem to think I have something to do with her disappearance."

"And did he—help you to find Becky?"

Tree shook his head. "You say Georgi is missing. They told me at the bar that he's dead."

"Then what did you do?"

"What could I do? I was with my associate, Gladys Demchuk, and together we drove back to Fort Myers."

Drew leaned forward, speaking intently, "Tree, never mind what we may or may not think about you. Not only are you interfering with an ongoing federal investigation, but if you're trying to prove your innocence, you are doing just the opposite, making yourself look more guilty, not less."

"What does that mean? Is it time to call my lawyer?"

Drew gave him an impatient look. "Help me out, Tree. Show me some good faith. Tell me what it is you're not telling me."

Like Becky McPhee holding the gun that may have killed Yuri Revin? Such as Georgi, the previously rescued Russian gangster, now the disappeared Russian gangster? Yes, there were a few things Tree could come clean about as long as he was ready to spend the next twenty years or so in a federal prison.

That is, if the world didn't end first.

"There is nothing I have to say," Tree answered at last. That was at least partially true.

"Here's the thing, Tree. At every turn in this investigation, I find you standing there, whether it's with Becky before she disappears, your ex-wife mixed up with a missing Russian cosmonaut who was involved with Becky, or outside a club belonging to a missing Russian gangster who is the uncle of the missing cosmonaut who was involved with the missing Becky."

"Nothing more than coincidences," Tree said.

"I think you're lying. Lying through your teeth. Lying to a federal agent is about as bad, if not worse, than *not* lying to a federal agent."

"Which is why I'm not lying to you," Tree said. There was what he could say, and then there was what he was *willing* to say. The truth resided in the part he was willing to say, thus, he hoped, avoiding jail time.

At least for now.

Drew was on her feet. "I repeat: I believe you are lying." Her suspicious eye fell on Freddie. "Ms. Stayner, I hope that you are not complicit in what your husband is up to. I would hate to see you in as much trouble as he is."

"I am merely an innocent bystander," Freddie said, taking on an innocent bystander's expression of innocence.

Drew commented on the statement with a baleful look.

Tree said, "Agent Castle, you mentioned something earlier about Valentin being involved with Judy Markov."

"Did I?"

"Tell me how you think they are involved."

"Don't tell me there is something you don't know about your ex-wife?"

"There is plenty I don't know about my ex-wife," Tree said.

"What do you say we make a deal, Tree? You give me something. I give you something. Until then, I don't have anything more to tell you."

Tree followed her to the door. A short woman next to Tree, she paused at the threshold, seeming to vibrate with aggressive, intimidating energy. "Listen to me, Tree, I know all about your interactions with the local cops over the years. And I know you've had a few unpleasant brushes with the FBI. You've gotten away with a lot of shit you shouldn't have gotten away with. But that was before you met me. I don't stop. I don't take any crap from anyone. You jerk me around and I swear you will end up in a federal prison. Think about that. I will give you one last chance after today to come clean. Otherwise, so help me God, I will drop the hammer on you."

She went out into the sunshine. Tree watched her get into her vehicle before he closed the door and turned to find Freddie standing there. "She scares me," Freddie said.

"Does she?"

"A pint-sized, one-eyed FBI agent threatening to put you in prison for the rest of your life, yeah, that scares me."

Tree didn't want to say anything, but she scared him too.

30

"Go away, Tree." Judy's annoyed voice sounded muffled coming from the intercom at the front gate of her house.

Tree leaned further out the window of the Mercedes and said, "I'm not going away, Judy. You lied to me."

"What did I lie to you about?"

"You said you didn't know Valentin Baturin."

"You are not coming in here. Didn't you see the sign? 'No ex-husbands allowed.'"

"I can either talk to the police about what I know or I can talk to you. For the time being, anyway, and for some strange reason, I'd rather talk to you. But if the police know what I know then they'll be around to find out what you know—and believe me, that's not going to go well for either one of us."

"I love it when you turn up threatening me," Judy said, sounding like she didn't love it at all.

The intercom clicked off. In the silence that followed, Tree started to think Judy wasn't kidding, that she was not about to let him in. And then as if some telepathic power was at work between Tree and his ex-wife, unseen machinery whirred into action and the gate opened. A stone-faced guard waved him on through.

Judy was stationed on the front steps as though to block any attempt by Tree to get inside. Just in case he made a try, two beefy, stone-faced security people kept an eye on him.

Tree parked and then got out of the car and walked toward Judy, keeping his hands where the security guys could see them.

"What is it now?" Judy demanded.

"I thought I'd drop by after spending time with an FBI agent threatening to put me in prison and throw away the key."

"Am I supposed to think that's bad news?"

"What will save me, is what I've learned over the years when it comes to dealing with the feds."

"And what is that?"

"I talk, tell them things that they think I know."

"And that gets you out of trouble, does it?"

"It does, usually."

"What is it you know that would interest the FBI?"

Tree jerked a thumb in the direction of the Mercedes. "That Mercedes over there," he said.

"Yes, a Mercedes," Judy agreed impatiently. "You drive a Mercedes, good for you, although why do I suspect it belongs to your wife? What about it?"

"You know that Becky drove off with it last night outside Everglades City after Freddie and I tried to help her. For some reason that you may want to explain to me, she drove here."

"That's ridiculous," Judy asserted. "I have no idea what you're talking about."

"Becky was smart enough to know she couldn't hold on to the car, and she probably worried that I would report it stolen. But she would have no idea where I lived. However, you do know—and lo and behold the Mercedes ends up back in my driveway this morning."

"An interesting story, but it has nothing to do with me," Judy stated. "Although, for Freddie's sake, I am glad that if your car was stolen last night, it has been returned to you."

"Either Becky is inside or she was here and you know where she is."

"I have often wondered in the years since we were together how I could ever have been so naïve and young as to marry a crazy individual such as yourself. Now again today, hearing these preposterous accusations, I am left to wonder all over again. How utterly stupid I must have been."

"I prefer to think of you as an intelligent woman who many years ago was swept off her feet by my irresistible charm."

"I prefer to think I was stupid."

"Why don't I talk to the FBI, tell them what they want to hear about what's happened to Becky? Let's see if they agree that I'm as crazy as you seem to think."

"You do keep threatening me, don't you?"

"Yes, I do."

"What do you want, Tree? You must want something. You always do."

"I'd like to know why you lied about being associated with Valentin Baturin."

"I'm not sure I did lie. I may have dodged the truth a bit."

"Why would you do that?"

"How would you know I'm associated with him?"

"Put it this way, amid all the threats from the FBI as they attempted to find out what I know, they inadvertently told me something useful."

Judy hesitated, seeming to gather her thoughts before she said, "Several years ago, I invested in Russia's space program, principally through a private company, RKK Energiya. As you can imagine, launching rockets into space isn't something I know much about. I needed someone who understood Russia's space industry and could guide me through what turned out to be a byzantine business. Valentin was suggested."

"What about Yuri Revin?"

Judy said nothing, but the twitch of that pink bow of a mouth gave her away. "As far as I know, Yuri is a part of the Russian space program. Valentin introduced us. They're friends."

"Is he sleeping with Becky?"

Judy looked suddenly impatient. "Here's the thing, Tree. The FBI isn't who should concern you. At the end of the day, you'll be fine. As far as they're concerned, you are nothing more than a dumb, aged private detective who doesn't know much of anything."

"Thanks a lot," Tree said.

"If I were you—and thank God, I'm not—I would keep my nose out of this. If, of course, you don't want to get that nose and a few other things, broken."

"Now you're threatening me."

"What do you know? It looks like I am."

"I may have mentioned this before, but one of my problems is that I have trouble deciding what's good for me."

"One of your many problems," Judy said. "This time you better decide fast. Otherwise, I can't be responsible for what happens."

"I'm having a hard time deciding who I should be more afraid of: Georgi Zhukov, the FBI, or you."

"You just don't get it, do you, Tree?"

"Tell me, Judy, what is it I don't get?"

"You idiot, the person you should truly be afraid of is the person who hired you in the first place."

31

FIVE DAYS BEFORE THE END OF THE WORLD

The big white TV trucks still clustered on Captiva Drive across from Palm Flower Lane, but most reporters and photographers had disappeared. The Becky McPhee story, while hardly ignored on front pages and on the twenty-four-hour cable newscasts, had fallen into a kind of rhythm with the realization that in all likelihood Becky wasn't going to show up at the front gate, and therefore the media's resources—already stretched thin in this journalistically challenged age—could best be allocated elsewhere.

At least that was the theory Tree played out to himself hunkered in the Mercedes parked on the oceanside further along Captiva. Sitting there with a good view of Palm Flower Lane, he tried not to think about the ridiculousness of staking out the man who had hired him in the first place. He doubted confronting Dwight McPhee would accomplish much, providing he would even be admitted back into McPhee world. If Judy was right and Dwight McPhee was the real threat, then what? What had he been missing?

Maybe a little distance would help. If he could stay awake.

An hour or so later, his sleepy persistence was somewhat rewarded when a red sports car, its canvas top in place, sped onto Captiva from Palm Flower Lane. Miranda McPhee, her face mostly hidden behind dark glasses and shadowed by the peak of a baseball cap, was behind the wheel.

Tree started up the Mercedes and then eased out onto the roadway in pursuit.

Miranda crossed Blind Pass onto Sanibel, taking the winding back route, turning onto West Gulf Drive to avoid the congestion on Periwinkle Way.

She drove as far as Lindgren Boulevard before turning left to rejoin Periwinkle. From there it was an easy ride onto the causeway, Tree keeping two or three cars behind.

Once off the island, Miranda kept going straight onto Summerlin Road. She drove as far as San Carlos then made a right turn onto the boulevard. With Tree increasingly mystified as to where she was headed, he followed her south on San Carlos. He was starting to think she must be bound for Fort Myers Beach when she abruptly slowed and turned into the Bright Sunshine Trailer Court, a recreational vehicle park. Tree had no choice but to drive on. A short distance away, he was able to turn into the parking lot at Sun Homes Services. The lot was almost empty as he came to a stop.

Tree left the car and walked back to Bright Sunshine. A hodgepodge of aluminum-sided mobile homes jammed between San Carlos and the waters of Hurricane Bay, shiny under an unremitting sun that drove residents indoors so that the place seemed eerily deserted.

Tree came along the roadway that intersected the park, wondering how he would find Miranda. Then he spotted her sports car. It was parked beside a battered gray-sided trailer with a slanted roof, fronted by a patch of grass. A cluster of palm plants obscured the single window. A white-framed screen door was built into the addition that had been added as an afterthought.

Tree stood in front of the trailer considering his next move.

To hell with it, he thought, and pounded on the aluminum frame of the entrance door.

Almost immediately the door opened to reveal Miranda, naked except for a pair of black-lace panties, her welcoming smile evaporating as soon as she saw who it was. "Jesus Christ!" she exclaimed.

She tried to close the door but Tree got his foot in the way. "I think we'd better talk," he said to her. "Why don't you put something on?"

Her eyes flashed in a face full of fury. She turned away to a red sofa where the white T-shirt she had been wearing lay. Tree waited by the door until she shrugged into it and then flopped down on the sofa, crossing her bare legs, rubbing at her arms. "What the hell do you want?"

"Like I said, some talk." Tree had stepped inside, closing the door behind him. Faux wood paneling was on the walls, a red armchair matched the red sofa flanked by white-shaded lamps mounted on end tables. A glass-topped coffee table stood in front of the sofa. Not Miranda's style, Tree thought, but apparently it would do for what she had planned this afternoon.

"He's going to be here shortly, and when he sees you he's going to kill you." She practically hissed the words.

"Then let's not waste time." Tree showed her the three photos he had found in the cabin outside Everglades City. Slack-jawed, Miranda permitted herself a glance at them and then quickly pulled her eyes away.

"Look, I don't know what you're up to," she said angrily, "but I don't have to tell you shit. Chip says you're nothing more than a stupid local private eye in over his head. I'm beginning to think he is right."

"Tell me about Yuri," Tree said.

"Yuri is a bastard," she said with a shrug. "He announces he's madly in love with my sister, the world-famous astronaut, and he can't live without her and all this other crap. He even cheated his friend Valentin to get at her."

"Becky left Valentin for Yuri?"

"I'm not sure Becky 'left' Valentin. But one way or another she ended up dumping Valentin for Yuri although I'm not sure what she saw in him."

"What did you see in him?"

"A chance to get back at my sister?" Miranda shrugged. "Maybe that had something to do with it, who knows? But the thing is, after all his protestations of love, it took Yuri about two seconds before he was in bed with me. I guess I wasn't taking it all that seriously, but then he thought he was. Suddenly, he couldn't live without *me*. Well, that got to be too much so I broke it off. But that was easier said than done. He kept phoning, driving me crazy."

"Does your sister know about the two of you?"

"Put it this way. She might know it's the end of the world, but she doesn't know about Yuri and me. At least I don't think she does."

"Would Becky have disappeared to be with Yuri?"

"You'd have to ask my sister, but, yeah, I suppose that could explain a lot of things, couldn't it? I certainly haven't heard from Yuri for a while—thank goodness."

She sauntered toward Tree, making it obvious she had nothing under her T-shirt. Tree thought fleetingly of all those pulp detective novels he had read as a kid wherein the hero finds himself contemplating the femme fatale in the same manner he now looked at Miranda. She smirked, knowing where his eyes were focused. "How about giving me those photos?" she purred. "You certainly don't need them."

"What's going on, Miranda?" Tree demanded. "Where's your sister?"

"Don't tell me you followed me here because you think I know something?" She smiled and tossed her hair around.

"The night Becky disappeared, when we were at your father's house. You came in and told me I was being set up. What did you mean?"

"I must have been drunk when I said that. Or else I said it before I learned to keep my mouth shut."

"You also said your brother was murdered."

"Nothing so dramatic, I'm afraid," Miranda said sadly. "Tad simply killed himself."

"Or have they taught you to keep your mouth shut about that, too?"

"Man, you really are grasping at straws. We've all been set up when it comes down to it. My sister's crazy and now we're caught up in her craziness. She was crazy before she ever went into space, crazy enough to join the Navy SEALs of all things—and certainly crazy enough to believe she heard voices telling her the world is coming to an end."

"Crazy enough to fake her own disappearance?" Tree asked.

The question actually wiped the smirk off Miranda's face and caused her to purse her lips in contemplation. "I don't know about that," she admitted. "My thinking is that even Becky is not *that* crazy, but I don't know."

"What about your father?"

"You mean is he nuts too? Yeah, probably. Nuts enough to still love your wife after all this time."

"Does he?"

"You know it's true. How do you like that?"

"Not very much," Tree said.

"Tell you what. Give me those photos, and I'll let you in on what my father has planned for your wife."

"Does he have something planned?"

She held a slim hand out. "The photos. And I will tell all."

"For now, I'll hang onto them."

Her clear face darkened; any sense of seduction had disappeared. "You're a bastard," she said.

"That's what everyone keeps telling me," Tree said.

"Everyone is right," Miranda said as he started for the door.

The trailer door opened. Chip Holbrook worked through various expressions of anger and confusion as he spotted Tree.

32

What the hell?" he breathed. He seized Tree by the shirt-
front, lifting him off his feet and out the door, throwing
him down on patchy grass.

"What do you think you're doing?" Chip was breathing
hard as he leapt down the steps to deliver a hard kick to Tree's
ribs.

Miranda was poised in the doorway. Tree could dimly hear
her shouting, "Get the photos!"

That momentarily distracted Chip. He paused his kicking.
"What?"

"He's got photos. Get them!"

"You bastard! You trying to blackmail my girl?" Chip resumed kicking. Tree began to view the world through a galaxy
of blurry stars. He tried rolling away but Chip was much too
fast. He yanked Tree to his feet and shoved him back against
the side of the mobile home, trampling the palm plants in the
process.

Chip was tearing at Tree's pockets when someone struck
him on the side of the head. Chip staggered away, wobbled a
bit and then fell to the ground, holding his bleeding head.

Nino gripped the tire iron he had used to whack Chip. He
was flanked by two of the refrigerators from Georgi's.

"Sorry pal," Nino said to Chip, tire iron at the ready in case
further blows were needed. "I get first dibs when it comes to
kicking the shit out of this asshole."

Miranda had begun to scream in the doorway. The two
refrigerators seized Tree and frog-marched him over to a white

panel van where the third refrigerator was opening the van's sliding side door. The two refrigerators threw him inside with much the same effort they would use to toss a sack of potatoes. Tree landed hard on the van's floor. Nino, his bleak, hollowed-out face alive with the excitement of the possible kill, arrived, replacing the tire iron with a Glock automatic that he pressed against Tree's forehead. "Just stay where you are, asshole, and as they say in the movies, don't move."

As soon as the two refrigerators crowded in, the side door of the van slammed shut. Nino got into the passenger seat as the refrigerator behind the wheel started the engine and then sped forward.

"If you're thinking we saved your ass or something like that—don't," Nino stated from the front, twisting to level the Glock at Tree. "You are out of the frying pan, amigo, and you are in the shit."

"Fire," Tree corrected.

Nino looked momentarily confused. "What?"

"It's out of the frying pan and into the fire."

"No, no," Nino countered. "There's no frying pan, my friend. You are deep in the shit—unless you help me out."

Tree had a sense of the van back on San Carlos Boulevard. "I'm not sure how I can help you," he ventured.

"Lucky for you, I can absolutely tell you how you help. You can tell me where I can find Georgi. That way you help me, and I help you by not blowing your brains out all over the inside of this van."

"Don't do that," advised Tree.

"Then tell me where Georgi is."

"That's easy enough," Tree said. "I have no idea where he is."

"I thought you didn't want me to blow your brains out."

Nino reached back so he could press the Glock's snout hard against Tree's skull.

"I don't," Tree said. "But what is it with the two of you, anyway?"

"Let's say it's a family feud," Nino said. "I'm young with plenty of energy, and I want to take over his business. He's old and has no energy at all and doesn't want me to take over his business. You can see the problem, right? Now tell me where I can find the old bastard."

"The last time I saw Georgi he was at my house on Captiva Island. Then he disappeared and I haven't heard from him since."

"What's the deal with you and him, anyway?" To Tree's relief, Nino had relaxed the gun against his head. "Why do you give a shit about the old fart? He would probably kill you as soon as look at you. He has no friends, no loyalty to anyone except himself."

"Let's say his nephew, Valentin, is a person of interest."

"Valentin? That prick? You go after my uncle to get to Valentin? You're wasting your time. You should have come to me."

"I did come to you."

"Okay, yeah, you got a point, I suppose. You sure you don't know where Georgi is?" By now, to Tree's further relief, Nino had removed the gun from the area around his head.

"I wish I did. I'd like to talk to him myself."

"Okay, here's the deal I'm gonna make with you. Simple, okay?"

"Let's hear the deal."

"You find Georgi and when you do, you let me know, okay? In return, I tell you where you can find Valentin."

"Are you sure he's still alive?"

Nino looked taken aback. "Is he alive? Of course, he's alive. Why would that prick be anything else?"

"No one seems to be able to find him."

"We got a deal or not?"

"What are you going to do with Georgi if I help you find him?"

"Hey, he's my uncle, okay? We talk. I make him listen to reason. He's a stupid old fart so he doesn't listen. But eventually he comes around."

"You're not going to kill him?"

"Kill my uncle? How can you even think such a thing?"

"It might have something to do with that garage you were holding him in, wrapped in duct tape."

"Yeah, okay. But I didn't *kill* him—and I won't. Not unless he tries to kill me first."

"All right. Where can I find Valentin?"

"Okay, I don't know where he is."

"Then how can we have a deal?"

"The thing is, I *do* know where he is—sometimes."

"Where is that?"

"You go up to Bokeelia on Pine Island. You go to a place along the water called The Jug Creek Boathouse. You go in there. If Valentin isn't already there, he's gonna show up any time."

"Why would Valentin be up at Bokeelia?"

"What can I tell you? The guy's a prick, like I said. I guess he loves it up there or something. He says it's the only place in the world where he can relax and no one bothers him."

"Okay," Tree said, not certain Nino wasn't sending him on a wild goose chase.

"But you'd better hurry up, my friend, you don't have much time."

"What do you mean?"

"Shit, man, haven't you heard?" Nino said with a laugh. "It's the end of the friggin' world."

He turned and called to the refrigerator driving the van. "Hey, Viktor, slow it down, will you?"

Immediately Viktor slowed. Nino said to Tree, "Hey, you don't forget our deal, okay? You forget the deal, and it's the frying pan and a lot of shit. Okay?"

"Sure, I understand," Tree said. "Are you going to drive me home?"

Nino flashed a smile. "Are you friggin' kidding me? What do we look like? Uber? No, man, we won't be driving you home."

He nodded to one of the nearby refrigerators. He yanked at the latch on the side door. It slid open.

The other refrigerator grabbed Tree and again like a sack of potatoes, tossed him out of the moving van.

33

Tree lay still, trying to figure out whether he was conscious or unconscious, alive or dead. As he lay there, he ruled out dead since when he opened his eyes, he could see blue sky and hear the sounds of distant traffic. Unless he was mistaken, there wouldn't be any traffic in heaven. Would there? Of course, there was another possibility, that he was dead not in heaven, but rather in a place where there was traffic.

By now he had also surmised that in addition to being more or less alive he was also at least semiconscious. He knew this because of the pain beginning to send familiar shock waves through his body. He was alive, conscious, and facing the prospect of having broken every bone in said body.

He managed to get himself into a sitting position, discovering that he had ended up in a ditch adjacent to a shopping mall. He could see a Target store in the distance. Close by, a bus stop with a bench was occupied by a rail-thin black man. He wore a worn brown fedora, a short-sleeve Hawaiian shirt and a bemused expression on his gentle, weathered face. The thin man looked an awful a lot like the actor Morgan Freeman. "You all right there, partner?" he called as Tree tried to rise to his feet.

"I'm not sure," Tree answered. "I'm still trying to determine the damage." Tree peered at him. Was this the same thin man? The Morgan Freeman doppelganger in his dream? It was a dream, wasn't it?

"Have we met before?" Tree called to him.

"I dunno, partner. Have we?"

"I suppose people tell you how much you look like Morgan Freeman."

"All the time, partner. All the time."

The thin man stood to get a better view of the wounded stranger in the ditch. "I dunno, partner," he said with a shake of his head. "I've seen lots of things in my long years in this crazy state, but I ain't never seen anyone thrown out of a moving van before."

"Well, if you can possibly avoid it, I would suggest you stay away from the people who might throw you out of a van."

"Yeah, maybe it's just plain good luck on my part, but so far I've been able to do that."

Tree crawled out of the ditch, slipping once but then righting himself. He stood on the road shoulder, trying to catch his breath as he brushed the dirt off.

The thin man looked genuinely concerned. "Anything I can do to help?"

"No, I think I'm okay—more or less."

"You don't mind my saying, you seem a little old for these kinds of shenanigans."

"My wife thinks I should retire."

"Well, you maybe should listen to your wife."

"You know it's interesting," Tree said. "People tell me that all the time."

The thin man grinned. The years fell away. "But I guess you're a stubborn cuss, huh?"

"Stubborn or crazy, I'm not sure which."

"Any consolation, I've been accused of both stubborn and crazy over the years."

"You know, the last time we met, you told me the world really was going to end."

"I told you that?" The thin man looked surprised. "Well, sure, it's a possibility all right."

"You also told me I haven't measured up in my life."

"Yeah? I said that did I?"

"You did," confirmed Tree.

"I guess when it comes to measuring, we've all fallen short. Look at me. Here we are at the end and here I am still waiting for a bus."

Tree fished his cellphone out of his pocket. The fall had splintered the screen, but he was able to get a dial tone. He saw a local bus coming down the street. The thin man saw it too. "I'd better move, that's my bus. You sure you're gonna be all right?"

Tree nodded. "Thanks. I'm phoning my wife now."

"The one who keeps telling you to retire."

"That's the one."

"Well, you tell her you met Micah today, and he agrees with her."

"Micah?"

"That's me, partner."

"You sure we haven't met?"

"Well, I guess we've met now, haven't we? Don't forget to tell your wife."

"I'll do that, Micah."

The bus had drawn to a stop. "Micah, that's an Old Testament name incidentally," the thin man called back as he headed for the bus. "Means 'who is like God.'"

"Are you like god, Micah?" Tree asked.

Micah grinned. He paused at the entrance to the bus.

"What do you think? Is the world coming to an end?" Tree called.

"Why not?" Micah had one foot on the step. "Everything

comes to an end, partner. You. Me. Everything. Why not the world?"

"I knew it," Tree called. "We *have* met before."

Micah waved and then hopped into the bus. The doors closed. The bus moved off down the street. Tree felt suddenly woozy. Every part of his body was in agony as he managed to make his way to the bus stop bench and fall onto it. He got Freddie on the phone.

"I just got thrown out of a van," he reported.

"You were driving the Mercedes, how did you get thrown out of a van?"

"I wasn't in the Mercedes."

"I got that part. Where is the Mercedes?"

"I said I got thrown out of a van. A moving van. Aren't you worried about me?"

"I'm more worried about the car."

"It's outside a trailer park."

Tree heard Freddie heave a sigh. "Okay, stay put. Where are you?"

"San Carlos, I believe. There's a mall with a Target store."

"I'll Uber over there," Freddie said.

"You're an angel," Tree said.

The line went dead.

The battered warrior home, showered, an ice pack applied to swelling bruises, pleas to get checked out at emergency for more broken parts. and finally, the usual expressions of dismay around how the warrior could once again get himself so banged up.

"It's not easy," Tree said once Freddie had him settled more or less comfortably on the terrace, ice pack in place, the dying evening sun warming his aching bones. "First of all, you have to be kicked around by an ex-Navy SEAL then you have to allow yourself to be kidnapped by Georgi's power-hungry nephew, and when he's finished with you, get thrown out of a moving van."

"Tree, for God's sake," said Freddie in astonishment. "You're lucky you didn't break every bone in your body."

"The jury is still out as to whether I did or did not," Tree replied. "The way I'm feeling at the moment, I'm leaning toward 'did.'"

He proceeded to fill Freddie in on the day's events: following Miranda to her mobile trailer assignation with a lover who turned out to be Chip Holbrook, the Navy SEAL who didn't like finding Tree with Miranda.

Showing Miranda the photographs he found inside Yuri Revin's wallet didn't particularly upset her, Tree reported. She had begun an affair with him then dropped him. He had been following her around being a pain about the end of their affair.

"Then Miranda doesn't know that Yuri is dead," said Freddie.

"She probably wouldn't care much even if she did."

"Anything else?"

"Nino, Georgi's nephew, who before he launched me out of his van, swore that Valentin is hiding out at a bar in Bokeelia."

"Bokeelia? On Pine Island? What's he doing up there?"

"That," said Tree, "is what I intend to find out."

"Tree, you should be going to the hospital. You should not drive to Bokeelia."

"Given the choice between a hospital or Bokeelia, I prefer Bokeelia."

Freddie rolled her eyes, a reaction to his assertions that she had cultivated over the years.

"Besides," Tree went on, "there is not much choice. I've got the FBI breathing down my neck thinking I'm somehow involved in Becky's disappearance. And then there is a dead man outside Everglades City who is only going to get me in more trouble once someone finds his body."

"If you're going up there then I'm coming with you," Freddie said. "And don't tell me I can't go because it's too dangerous."

"I wasn't going to say that," Tree said.

"What were you going to say?"

"I was going to ask you to drive because I'm too banged up to get behind the wheel."

"Aha! There you go trying to outwit me again."

"Impossible," Tree stated. "However, there is a tiny problem we're going to have to deal with."

"What's that?"

"The Mercedes?"

Freddie groaned. "Anything happens to that car, I'm going to kill you," she said.

"Get in line," Tree advised. "My likely killers are lined up for miles."

"While we're in the process of irritating one another..." Freddie allowed the sentence to trail off.

"Are we in the process of irritating one another?"

"We might be," she said. "I had lunch today with Dwight McPhee."

"You had lunch with your old boyfriend," Tree clarified.

"I'm not sure I'd go that far," Freddie said.

"As far as old boyfriend or lunch?"

"The old boyfriend. I'm not so sure he was ever a boyfriend, whatever that means."

"Both his daughters told me you were the love of their father's life," Tree said.

"I don't believe that," Freddie said.

"That's what they said."

"That certainly wasn't how I felt about Dwight."

"What made you decide to have lunch with him?"

"I didn't decide anything. Dwight called and said he'd like to get together. For old time's sake."

"Ah, yes," Tree said. "That time-honored excuse for attempting to reignite former flames—old times' sake."

"Apparently, he remembers those times a lot better than I do," Freddie said. "But I decided to meet with him thinking I might learn something if it was just the two of us."

"And did you—learn anything?"

"If I'm honest, I would have to say no, not really. However, he did give me the impression of being a lot more interested in me than in his daughter's disappearance or the fact that his son has recently died from a drug overdose."

"Anything else?"

"You're not going to like this," Freddie said.

"Tell me anyway, please."

"Dwight admitted that part of the reason he hired you was so he could meet me again."

"You're right," Tree said. "I don't like that, although it's not the first time that observation has been made."

"My goodness," Freddie said. "I do believe you are jealous."

"Not me," Tree said, without sounding the least bit convincing. "How could I ever be jealous?"

She came over to the chaise lounge and embraced him. "You fool…"

"Careful," he said. "Every bone in the fool's body aches."

"You know I love you."

"Even though I'm poor and can hardly move?"

"Even though," Freddie said before she kissed him. Then she pulled away, suddenly pensive.

"What?" he asked.

"Like I said, I didn't really learn anything, but still…It's hard to explain, that lunch…"

"What about it?"

"Something…something about him…Something wasn't right."

"What do you mean?"

"I don't know, but something…call it intuition, whatever…but something…"

34

FOUR DAYS BEFORE THE END OF THE WORLD

NPR reported that with days left before the solar eclipse, police and FBI continued their search for the missing astronaut, Becky McPhee.

The search was being led by FBI Special Agent Drew Castle. "We're working on a number of leads," the agent told NPR. "That's all I have to say for the moment."

Asked if she believed Becky was still alive, Special Agent Castle said that she "remained optimistic the missing astronaut will be found."

Meanwhile as the clock counted down to the eclipse, forest fires burned out of control in California and Australia. Hurricanes raged up the East Coast flooding the Carolinas and New England, moving relentlessly northeast toward New York. There was unusual tornado activity in the South and Midwest. Once again there was a run on gas, although it was observed that if the world really was coming to an end, a full gas tank wasn't going to help much.

People were said to be storing water in big wooden barrels and stocking nonperishable food items. Since there would be no electricity at the world's end and therefore all electronic devices would be useless, everyone was buying up batteries.

The wealthy, if they hadn't already, were rushing to complete work on their panic rooms. A California-based company whose motto was, "It's been predicted and you must prepare," was offering bunkers buried in a secret location in the mountains of the Sierra Madre for two hundred thousand dollars a bunker. Each bunker was built to withstand 450-mph winds, a magnitude 10 earthquake, fifteen days of 1,250 F surface fires, and one month of flooding.

The company said the bunkers had sold out.

———

Despite Freddie's dark mood the next morning, her grumbling that the Mercedes was not her husband's to constantly lose, Tree was able to convince her to join him in an Uber drive back to the Bright Sunshine Trailer Court.

He breathed a sigh of relief as he spotted the Mercedes where he had left it in the parking lot adjacent to the trailer court. "The marriage is saved—for now," Freddie announced.

With Freddie driving, it took them just over an hour to reach Bokeelia at the northern tip of Pine Island. Freddie drove in along Stringfellow Road and then turned left onto Main Street.

The Jug Creek Boathouse was just that, a converted boathouse jutting perilously into Charlotte Harbor, its rough plank siding weathered and worn, testament to its many years of storms endured. The boathouse opened to a wide sunlit terrace. The sun wasn't allowed inside. In the dim interior, the bartender with his white beard, bald head, and tattooed arms, had been sent over by central casting. He moved back and forth in time to a Garth Brooks song as Freddie and Tree entered.

The bartender's gaze immediately focused on Freddie as she perched on one of the stools. "Name's Mel," the bartender said in the kind of gruff tone expected from a central casting bartender with a bald head and a white beard. "What can I get you little lady?"

Tree slipped onto the stool beside Freddie, but he didn't exist. Freddie asked for a glass of chardonnay which caused Mel to wrinkle his nose. "Char-don-aaay..." he pronounced disdainfully. "Afraid all we got is white wine."

"Then I'll take your finest white wine." Freddie delivered the announcement with one of her winning smiles.

"House plonk, I'm afraid," said Mel.

"Bring it on," said Freddie.

Mel's contempt was more pronounced when Tree ordered a Diet Coke. On the sound system, Dolly Parton plaintively singing "I Will Always Love You," replaced Garth.

"Mel!" A rough rasp of a voice shouted out from somewhere in the back. "Turn that goddamn sad shit off!"

Mel placed a tumbler containing some sort of pale liquid in front of Freddie. The Diet Coke was plunked down in front of Tree.

"Mel!" the raspy voice called again.

"That's enough, Bear!" Mel shouted back in a rasp just about as rough. He shrugged and addressed Freddie. "That's Bear. He can be a pain in the ass."

Tree twisted around on his stool. In the feeble light, he could just make out someone at a table against the wall.

"You folks tourists?" Mel addressed Freddie.

"Not us," Freddie said. She lifted her glass. "We heard about the fine wine available at the Boathouse, and thought we'd drive up here and try it for ourselves."

"Yeah, folks come from all over the world for our wine," Mel said.

"In addition to the wine, we also heard we might find an old friend hanging out here."

"What kind of old friend would that be?" asked Mel.

"An old friend by the name of Valentin. Do you know him?"

"Valentin?" Mel shook his head. "Don't know anyone by that name."

"Like I said, he supposedly hangs out here," Freddie said.

"Lot of people hang out here, although not so much lately what with one thing and another."

"Mel! Turn that goddamn crap off!"

"Course, there's Bear," Mel said. "He's around here rain or shine—unfortunately."

Bear? Tree thought. He turned again, squinting, trying to get a better look at the customer named Bear.

"Mel! For the sake of heaven, man! That woman is *shit*!"

The song came to its stirring end. Silence fell across the Boathouse interior. Tree got off the stool and started toward the back. Mel called after him, "Don't know where you're headed, fella, but if I were you, I'd stay away from Bear."

Tree kept walking. He heard Freddie say, "Tree…"

The light shifted and the dimness lifted a bit so that by the time he got to the table where Bear was seated with a pitcher of draft beer, Tree had a much better view of him.

"What the goddamn hell you looking at?" Bear demanded, sounding not only gruff but also threatening.

"I guess I'm looking at you, Valentin…" Tree said.

35

A more corpulent Valentin certainly; a Valentin with an unkempt beard and long blondish brown hair pushed back from his forehead; a flush-faced Valentin; a Valentin with a drunk's watery, red-rimmed eyes.

But Valentin. Even in the uncertain barroom light, Valentin.

"It's Bear," Valentin said. "Don't call me Valentin."

Tree eased into the chair on the other side of the table as he said, "I'm W. Tremain Callister. Everyone calls me Tree. I'm a private detective around these parts."

Valentin allowed those watery drunk's eyes to focus on Tree, but he said nothing.

"You're a hard man to find," Tree said.

"This is for the simple reason I don't want to be found. You don't want to be found? You wish to wait for the end of the world in peace and quiet? You come to Bokeelia. You come to Bokeelia to die."

"Is that why you're here?"

"We are all going to die. Some of us wish to die in Bokeelia."

"What about Yuri Revin?"

"My so-called friend." Valentin's voice was full of contempt.

"But now he is dead."

The tightening of his jaw was the only sign of emotion Valentin allowed. "Yuri is also stupid. Stupid gets you killed in this world, even as it comes to an end."

"Becky was there when I found Yuri."

Valentin didn't respond.

"She drove off that night. I've been trying to find her."

Valentin laughed mirthlessly and made a throwaway gesture with his hand. "The world looks for Becky. What do you think, my friend? You believe she really heard the Voice?"

"What do you think?"

"Becky hears a voice in space, there is *reason* why she hears this voice. Becky never does anything unless there is a *reason* for it. She is crafty, that one, let me tell you."

"Any idea what that reason might be?"

Valentin sat back, took his time considering Tree's question. "What makes you think I have any interest at this point in understanding Becky? I have tried many times, it doesn't work. You do not understand, Becky. You merely accept her and stay out of her way. Come to think of it, maybe that is why I am in Bokeelia."

"Here is my thinking," Tree said, leaning forward.

"*Your* thinking," Valentin said with a snort of laughter.

"After Becky shot Yuri—"

"Becky did not shoot Yuri." Valentin's pronouncement was decisive.

"Yes, she told me she didn't so maybe she was telling the truth. Let's assume that. She drove off, running away from the murder scene. But where was she going to go? Maybe she needed someone who loved her, someone she had betrayed and wanted to make amends to. She came looking for the man she affectionately called Bear. She knew how you felt about Bokeelia, that this was your way of escape. She could find you here. And maybe she could find some peace and quiet for herself."

"The private detective at work, thinking things through, impressive," Valentin said. "I like that, Mr. Tree. There is only one problem."

"What's that?"

"It is all bullshit. It has nothing to do with anything."

"No?"

"Becky is not here."

"Do you know where she is?"

The question appeared to tire Valentin. He leaned back against the wall. His eyes narrowed, looking at something far away from Tree. "You know what? The Bear is tired of answering questions. If Becky wants to be found, she will be found. If she doesn't…" he shrugged. "What difference does it make? The world comes to an end soon, anyway."

"But you know where she is," Tree persisted.

"Go away," Valentin said with a wave of his hand. "The Bear don't want to talk to you."

"Hey, fella!"

Tree turned to Mel calling out from behind the bar. "You heard the man. He's through with you. *Vamos!*"

Freddie had come off the bar stool. "I think it's time we were going."

Tree rose to his feet. He wanted to say something more. But what?

Valentin seemed oblivious to everything—until he saw Freddie backlit by the light seeping in from the terrace. His dull eyes suddenly sparkled. He gave her a lazy smile. "What do we have here?" he asked. "Don't tell me you're with this guy?"

"I'm afraid so," Freddie said.

"Too bad I am in the process of nursing a broken heart, can't listen to that Dolly Parton shit," Valentin said. "Otherwise, it would be my pleasure to play Dolly and chase you around Bokeelia."

"That's not very far to chase," Freddie said. "But I do like Dolly."

The lazy grin widened. "I am getting old. I don't have the stamina I once had. Besides, I've discovered it is hard to chase women when your heart is broken."

"Mind if I ask who broke your heart?"

"Maybe you," Valentin said.

"I would definitely have broken your heart twenty years ago," Freddie said. "Now, probably not."

The twinkle of interest in Valentin's eyes brightened more. "Don't be so sure—"

"Fredryka," Freddie said.

"Yes…"

"Everyone calls me Freddie."

Valentin was sitting up now, alert. He spoke to Tree. "You should have sent Freddie to ask the questions," he said. "I like Freddie. I don't like you."

"Everybody likes Freddie," Tree said. "Nobody likes me."

"Tell me who broke your heart, Valentin," Freddie said.

"Our Lady of the Voices, who else?" he said dreamily. "She listens to a voice in space, but does not listen to me."

"There's more, isn't there?"

"Sit beside me, Freddie," Valentin said. "Comfort me in my time of need."

Freddie slipped onto the seat beside him. She leaned close, speaking to him in a low, understanding voice. "The man with Becky…"

"Yuri…Yuri," Valentin murmured. "My friend…her Yuri…"

"And she wouldn't listen," Freddie said.

"No…"

"When you realized, she wasn't listening to you…"

"To Yuri, now she listened to Yuri…" Valentin was sitting back with his eyes half closed, his voice seeming to float in the dreamy faraway.

"What did you do?" Freddie asked.

"Freddie, you are an intelligent woman. Tell me..." Valentin said.

"When you realized what he was doing to you, what Yuri was doing, his betrayal... That he was with Becky, not you..."

"It wasn't hard to find them. I knew where they were..."

"In Everglades City..."

"I do not die in Everglades City...but Yuri...He is scum. He goes to Everglades City to love—and to die..."

"When you got there, I imagine the place was in darkness. But you could hear them..."

"I heard them fighting. I saw her run out. I came up the stairs..."

"You had a gun with you," Freddie offered.

Valentin turned his head back and forth. "No, Yuri's gun... left on a table...foolish..."

"You were angry, not thinking straight," Freddie said. "Understandable.... the sense of betrayal, your friend..."

"The gun... on the table..."

"In the darkness, you shot Yuri," Freddie said softly. "Becky never knew..."

"I wanted to shoot her, but then I heard Dolly Parton...I would always love her, always...couldn't do it...dropped the gun to the floor..."

"And then you left, simply walked out of there," Freddie said. "You went down the steps and got into your car and drove away...kept driving until you got here."

Valentin closed his eyes tighter and said, "I die in Bokeelia."

He withdrew the gun that must have been on his lap all this time, the gun Tree hadn't noticed before now. He placed the gun on the table in front of him. His hand stayed on the gun. Beside him, Freddie stiffened.

"You don't need that," Freddie spoke calmly but she had noticeably tensed.

"I did not need the gun before," Valentin murmured. "But I need it now." He picked the gun off the table. "To die in Bokeelia…"

"Valentin…" Freddie's voice was even softer, edged with tension. "I hate to say this, but Bokeelia is no place to die."

"It is fine," he said with the beginnings of a smile. "I like you, Freddie, you understand. It is all right. In the end…"

"Yes, I do understand, Valentin. Why don't you put the gun down?"

Instead, Valentin rose from the table, the gun in his hand. Not pointing it at anyone, simply holding it.

"Valentin!" Mel had moved from the bar, seeing Valentin with the gun. "Whatever you're planning to do…"

"It is all good, Mel," Valentin said calmly. "You have been a fine host. A good place to have a quiet drink…to sit, to think… to remember…"

Valentin drifted out toward the deck. Freddie was on her feet following him as he went out into the sunshine and the heat.

He raised his head, blinking into the sun. Freddie advanced, followed by Tree and Mel, everyone moving in slow motion. "Valentin, please…" Freddie called in desperation.

Valentin lifted himself onto the low railing. A warm breeze sent his long hair swirling around his placid face. He cast a fond look at Freddie, frozen in mid step. "I could have loved you, Freddie," he said. "Everyone falls in love with you, don't they? How could they not?"

"Valentin, please, let me have the gun."

He didn't appear to hear her. "You needn't have come, though. You don't want me, I know; it is Becky but you are so far away…too far away."

"What do you mean?" Tree blurted out the words.

"You must look closer…closer to home," Valentin said. "You do not come to Bokeelia for love. You come for…"

He didn't finish the sentence. With his free hand he pushed the hair away so he could more easily place the snout of the gun into his opening mouth.

Freddie screamed. Valentin pulled the trigger.

36

It didn't take long before the local sheriff's department called the FBI. Impressively, Special Agent Drew Castle arrived by helicopter. The chopper landed in the parking lot at the bottom of the ramp leading to the Jug Creek Boathouse.

The deputies had moved Freddie and Tree along with Mel the bartender to a grassy park area overlooking the harbor. They kept Mel at a distance. He sat cross-legged on the grass, staring at the comings and goings of the various law enforcement officers, smoking cigarette after cigarette.

Tree sat on a bench with his arm around Freddie. There had been a lot of tears but by the time Special Agent Castle approached, Freddie had pulled herself together. Despite the late afternoon heat, Drew wore a blue windbreaker with FBI stenciled in big yellow letters on the back. Tree could see other agents kneeling to talk to Mel as he lit another cigarette and proceeded to blow smoke into the air.

"How are you two doing?" The question was grudging, an opening rather than any sincere expression of concern.

Tree and Freddie exchanged glances.

"Would you like to tell me what happened?"

Tree had spent much of the time as they awaited the arrival of authorities, trying to decide what to say. As he had so often in the past, he decided on a modified version of what could pass as the truth. Freddie said she was too exhausted to object. Tree must take the lead. He cleared his throat and then began by lying—or at least telling that modified version of the truth he had decided upon. He explained that as the result of a tip, he and Freddie had driven up to Bokeelia looking for Valentin—

"What do you mean a *tip?*" interrupted Drew.

"A tip from an informant I encountered while trying to find Becky," Tree explained.

He had barely got started on his explanation and already he had irritated Drew. "I told you before, Callister, you are not supposed to be *looking* for Becky McPhee. You are not supposed to be interfering with an FBI investigation."

"I understand that," Tree replied calmly. "Frankly, I didn't expect to find Valentin in Bokeelia. We came up here on a hunch, that's all."

"Who was this so-called informant?"

"For the moment, I can't give you that information," Tree said.

"And for the moment, I'm going to let that go," Drew said. "Continue with your story."

Tree told of how Valentin admitted to Freddie that he had shot his friend Yuri Revin when he discovered him with Becky in a house outside Everglades City."

"We found that body," Drew interrupted again. "We identified him as Yuri Revin, based on the identification that was at the scene. Becky and Revin were on the space station together. Maybe they developed a relationship there."

"Could be," Tree said.

"But then why would Valentin kill his friend, a fellow cosmonaut, then allow the woman who had betrayed him to live?"

"Dolly Parton," Freddie said.

"What?"

"He kept hearing Dolly Parton singing 'I Will Always Love You.' He couldn't bring himself to hurt her."

"What I don't understand is why Valentin would tell the two of you anything."

"Nothing to do with me, it was Freddie," Tree said.

Drew focused on Freddie. "Why you?"

"I think he was in turmoil over the loss of Becky and the murder of his friend. He wanted to get things off his chest before he died."

"You think he had been intending to kill himself?"

"He said he had come to Bokeelia to die. I just happened to be in a place where I was able to listen sympathetically."

"Valentin didn't happen to say where Becky is, did he?"

Freddie shook her head. "I'm afraid not."

Drew jerked a thumb in the direction of Mel and the other agents. "Our friend Mel over there knew where Valentin had rented a place nearby. The sheriff's department sent deputies around to have a look. No sign of Becky."

"I don't think she's been kidnapped," Tree said.

That didn't sit well with Drew. "How would you know that?" she demanded.

"Becky was able to get away to meet her lover. After Yuri was shot dead, why didn't she call the police? Why didn't she go home to her family? She didn't do any of that. She disappeared again. Where is she?"

"Be that as it may," Drew said curtly, "for now, we continue to treat this as a case of abduction."

"Time is running out," Freddie observed. "You had better hurry up and find her. Otherwise, the woman who predicted the end of the world may not be around for it."

No one said anything.

———

With Freddie still shaken, Tree drove back to Fort Myers. There was almost no traffic along Veterans Memorial Parkway at that hour. No sounds save for the swish of warm air against the car and the reassuring hum of the Mercedes' engine.

Finally, Freddie turned to her husband and said, "Say something."

"I was waiting for you," Tree said.

"You're the talker." Freddie's tone was surprisingly accusatory. "I'm not the talker, you are. You're the one who always has something to say. Say something."

"I'm sorry you were there and saw what you saw—obviously neither one of us knew what we were walking into."

Freddie remained silent. Tree cast a quick look at her. "But as awful as it was," he continued, "I'm glad you were there."

"You are? Why are you so glad?" Freddie's tone had turned hostile.

"Look, I know you're upset—I am, too. But thanks to you I'm in a little less trouble tonight than I was this morning."

"Because the FBI won't be coming after you for the murder of Yuri Revin? But what happens when they find out you tried to cover up our presence at that cabin outside Everglades City? What happens when they find out that you threw the murder weapon into the water? Are you still going to be in less trouble then? Or more?"

Now it was Tree's turn to grow silent.

"I hope it was worth it," Freddie continued. "That's all I'm saying. I hope it was all worth it."

"I don't know. Like you, I'm still processing what happened. We tried to stop Valentin. We couldn't—and we're both feeling like shit about it."

That drew more silence.

At last Freddie said, "Then there is what Valentin said just before he shot himself."

"Yes," Tree agreed.

"We are looking in the wrong place for Becky; we should be looking closer to home. Did you hear him say that?"

"Yes, of course I did."

"What did he mean?"

Tree kept driving.

"I'll tell you what it means, Tree. It means we're going in meaningless circles that aren't getting us anywhere. As for Valentin, you know what? I think he'd still be alive if we hadn't shown up."

"You don't know that," Tree said.

"Yes, I do." Freddie sounded adamant. "He confessed the murder of his friend to me. It was out there now, what was there left to do but take his own life? We made that happen—*I* made that happen, and I don't feel good about it."

"Let's just get home," Tree said quietly. "We can figure out the rest later."

They drove in silence.

It was almost dark as they pulled into Andy Rosse Lane. Tree felt something beyond exhaustion; an emptiness, drained of everything. Right now, he wanted only to get inside his house, wrap his arms around Freddie, try to bring her back from the dark place she was in. He was sure of this because emotionally, he was located right next door to her.

They came up the steps to the entrance and as they did, the front door opened. "There you are, finally!" boomed Georgi Zhukov. "Come in, come in," he motioned. "I have dinner ready for you!"

37

I had nowhere else to go!" exclaimed Georgi. He was wearing an apron, fussing in the kitchen, preparing, "*govjadina po Strogonovski*," he announced. "Otherwise known as beef Stroganoff. But not just any beef Stroganoff, *traditional* Russian beef Stroganoff."

In the face of the busy gangster-turned-chef, Freddie and Tree, stationed nearby, felt somewhat out of place in their own kitchen as Georgi sauteed onions in a saucepan.

"Now there is debate over whether mushrooms are part of the traditional dish," Georgi went on. "Not so. The mushrooms are an American addition. As a child growing up in Sviyazhsk, a beautiful town on the Volga founded by Ivan the Terrible, you should know, my mother never used mushrooms for her Stroganoff. We never *had* mushrooms."

"Where have you been?" demanded Tree in an attempt to take back some semblance of control.

"Ah, where have I been?" Georgi turned to Freddie lingering in the doorway. "What about you, Freddie? Do you prefer your beef Stroganoff with mushrooms?"

"I don't even like beef Stroganoff," Freddie said.

"How can you possibly say that?" said an astonished Georgi. "You will *love* my beef Stroganoff."

Tree said, "Georgi, please. Answer the question."

"Where have I been? Working very hard to take care of that lunatic, Nino."

"When you say, 'take care,' what's that mean?"

"Don't worry. For now, Nino's ass is safe." Georgi issued

a quick smile as he added sour cream to the simmering beef. "Alas, I could not find dry mustard in your cupboard, but I think it will be fine."

"Georgi," interrupted Tree. "What about Nino?"

"Yes, Nino. My plan did not quite work out the way I hoped. Which is why I am back here with you this evening, serving you my excellent beef Stroganoff, named, incidentally, after the great 19th Century statesman Count Pavel Alexandrovich Stroganov, although why he was so great and why anyone named a dish after him, remains a mystery to me."

He bent over a second saucepan containing potatoes that he had cut up. "Here in America, the Stroganoff is served with noodles or rice, but where I come from, potatoes are the traditional choice."

Georgi lifted up the saucepan to distribute the potatoes over the three plates he had already laid out on the counter. The Stroganoff followed. "I didn't use salt because I couldn't find any, which is a shame. But just the same, I believe it will be fine."

"What you're really telling us, Georgi," interjected Tree, "is that you are on the run with Nino out there looking for you."

"I would not be so melodramatic as to say I am 'on the run.' It is better to say I thought I should visit you, my good friends, and prepare a wonderful meal for the two of you."

"In other words, on the run," Freddie said.

"Come," said Georgi merrily, "let us eat together this wonderful meal I have prepared."

With little choice but to go along with this, the three of them ended up eating his beef Stroganoff down on the terrace, Georgi fussing, ensuring Freddie had wine, eagerly anticipating their reactions to his culinary creation. Freddie, who ordinarily stayed away from meat, had to admit the Stroganoff was "pretty good," a high compliment coming from her, Tree reassured a somewhat deflated Georgi.

As the meal finished, they related the news of the death of Valentin, Georgi adopting a sad expression that accompanied a much more pragmatic tone. "Unfortunate, certainly, but I never liked him, and yes, women will always drive you crazy, but please, you should never kill yourself because a woman betrayed you. Now Valentin did the right thing by shooting the duplicitous Yuri. But then to kill himself? No. This is not good."

Georgi sat back with a sigh. "We should not spoil a delicious meal on a lovely evening with all this talk of death."

"As the chef, perhaps you should be a little humbler when it comes to your own cooking," Freddie suggested.

"Yes, but I am not a humble person. I love to, as you say, blow my own horn? Yes, that's it. I love to do that—particularly when it comes to my skills in the kitchen."

"What about your skills when it comes to figuring out where Becky is?" Tree asked. "How are they?"

"Ah, Becky, Becky. Let me say this about Becky: if Becky has not been found until now, it is because she does not want to be found. No one has kidnapped her. No one holds her against her will. She simply has run away and does not wish to be found."

Freddie looked at Tree. "There is what Valentin said just before he died—that we were too far away. That if we were looking for Becky, we should be looking closer to home."

"What does that mean?" Georgi asked.

"For one thing it means what we already know, Becky is not in Bokeelia," Freddie said.

"Or Everglades City," added Georgi.

"Then where?" asked Freddie.

Tree thought about this for a time.

Freddie took notice. "I don't like it when you're thinking," she said.

Georgi gave her a bemused look. "You do not like your husband *thinking*?"

"It means we are soon going to get into a lot of trouble."

"There is something," Tree said.

"What is that?" asked Georgi.

"It would mean getting ourselves into the trouble Freddie mentioned—"

"There!" pronounced Freddie. "What did I tell you?"

"But if we do this right, we just might pull it off."

"Do what?"

He looked at Freddie. "I'm of two minds about what I need from you. On the one hand, this is something you may be eager to do. On the other hand, it could be something you refuse to go along with."

Freddie made a familiar groaning sound.

38

THREE DAYS BEFORE THE END OF THE WORLD

"Rex is going to kill me," Gladys said as she barreled down I-75 at her preferred rate of high speed. A speed that always made Tree nervous.

"You're going to kill us both if you don't slow down," Tree said.

"Hey, we don't have a lot of time to pull this off—that is if we can pull this off," she said.

"You have your doubts?"

"I have grave doubts," Gladys said. "But hey, let's give it the old college try."

She eased off the gas pedal. "There you go. I'm doing this for you."

"Much appreciated," Tree said.

"If you don't mind my saying, Tree, you're getting old," she added.

"You are right about that," Tree agreed. "I am getting old— and easily scared."

"A scaredy cat," she said.

"And, incidentally," he added, "the last thing Rex will do is kill you."

"The point is, I'm supposed to be answering the phone and helping him promote his book."

"How is that going?"

"Answering the phone or promoting the book?"

"Rex doesn't seem to be getting a lot of attention for his book."

"He thinks it's because I'm spending too much time schlepping you around."

"We should be back late this afternoon," Tree said reassuringly.

"I know you've been asked this many times by many people, myself included—"

"No," Tree interrupted, "I don't know what I'm doing."

Gladys allowed a slight smile. "Just wanted to check with you. You know, in case it turned out you have any idea what you are doing."

"Perish the thought," Tree said.

Her foot pressed down on the gas pedal. Tree gritted his teeth.

———————

There were no more patrons inside Georgi's late in the morning than there had been the last time Gladys and Tree visited. Which was to say there were no patrons at all. Frank, the bartender, was at his station behind the bar. If he recognized the two, he gave no sign of it. "What can I do for you folks?"

"We're looking for Nino," Tree said.

"You know, most people come in here for a drink," Frank observed.

"We're a little different," Gladys said. "We come in search of Nino."

"Yeah, well, Nino's not available."

"Tell Nino we can help him get to Georgi," Tree said. "But he's got to move fast."

Frank hesitated a bit before he said, "What makes you think Nino would be interested in Georgi?"

"Why don't we find out?" Tree said.

Frank waited a bit longer before he went down the bar and disappeared into the back. Gladys and Tree traded glances. "You didn't bring a gun with you by any chance?" he asked.

"Are you kidding?" Gladys opened her linen jacket enough to show him the stock of her 9 mm peeking above the belt of her jeans. "I never leave home without it," she said.

Nino, dressed in black in case anyone had doubts about his Russian gang affiliations, burst across the stage. He stopped at the stage's edge and Tree had a momentary thought that Nino might break into his rendition of "Oh What a Beautiful Morning."

He didn't.

"You're really pushing your luck," Nino said.

"You think so, Nino?" Was that a croak in his voice as he spoke? Gladys gave him a sharp look to confirm that it was.

Nino jumped down off the stage, "I gave you a pass the first time…"

"You pushed me out of a moving van and almost got me killed," Tree interjected.

"In the world I come from, that's a pass," Nino said. "The thing is, you're still alive and walking. You'd better have a pretty good excuse for why you and this lady are here—that is, if you want to continue living and walking."

"I've got a proposition for you," Tree said.

"Big deal," replied Nino.

"This big deal has to do with Georgi."

That brought a flicker of light into Nino's otherwise black eyes. "Yeah? What about him?"

"Supposing you could take him out of your life so that he wouldn't be coming after you anymore."

That produced a flash of anger. "Georgi's not coming after *me*; I'm coming after him."

"Supposing Georgi were to quietly retire and leave you to run things? What would you say to that?"

"I run things now," Nino asserted. His eyes narrowed. "Besides, he would never do that."

"Supposing he would?"

The flicker of interest had returned. "Why would he do something like that?"

"Because he and I need help and you're the only person who can provide the kind of help we both need."

"What guarantees do I have that he gets out?"

"Georgi is tired," Tree said. "Being away from all this, spending some quiet time with me and my wife has made him rethink things. He's willing to get out—he'll give you that guarantee in person. But he wants to be left alone."

"Yeah, that's all well and good," Nino said. "But I'm looking around here, and you know what? I don't see any sign of Georgi."

"You don't?" Tree turned and called out, "Georgi…"

The door opened and for a moment, the sunlight pouring in from outside was blocked by the dark form of Georgi Zhukov.

"Nino!" he exclaimed as the door swished shut behind him and he proceeded into the bar, throwing open his arms. "My favorite nephew! How are you, my friend? Are you well?"

"Jesus Christ," was all Nino had time to say before he was engulfed in his uncle's arms.

———

"It's a go with Georgi and Nino," Tree said when he phoned Freddie.

"You're sure about that?"

"Gladys and I are headed back with Georgi. Go ahead and make the call," Tree said.

"If you're absolutely sure…"

"It's fine, Freddie. Please. Make the call."

She waited a few minutes after Tree hung up, took a deep breath, and then called the number he had given her.

"I wondered if I would ever hear from you," Dwight McPhee said.

"I've debated whether to call or not," she said truthfully. "You know, given the circumstances."

"I understand, but I'm glad you called," he said. "How have you been?"

"Thinking more than I should about our lunch the other day."

"Me too," Dwight said.

"I'd like to talk. Somewhere private, you know, so we can just…talk…"

"Yes. I'd like that very much."

"This is a bit tricky," she said.

"Do you want me to suggest something?"

"No," she said quickly. "Here's the thing. A girlfriend of mine has gone up to Toronto for a couple of weeks. I'm checking on her house from time to time. I…I have a key…"

"All right, sure," Dwight said.

"We could meet there…it's private."

"Yes. Let's do that. When would you like to meet?"

She swallowed and said, "What about tomorrow afternoon? Or is that too soon?"

"No, no, that's good," he said immediately. "I just need a time and an address and I'll be there."

"How is three o'clock. That will give us time…"

"That's fine," he said.

"Dwight," she said. "It's important no one knows about this. I know it's difficult right now with all the attention…"

"Not to worry," he interrupted. "This is between us. I can get away all right. No one has to know."

She gave him the address and then hung up, feeling terrible.

But also, to her surprise, excited too.

39

TWO DAYS BEFORE THE END OF THE WORLD

The house sat on the edge of a canal. The living room looked out on the necessary swimming pool. Below the pool, a dock extended into the canal. The living room was serviceable enough for serviceable furniture. There was a serviceable kitchen off the serviceable living room. Freddie stood in the center of the room thinking of how typically Florida everything was, how monotonously similar to everything else, the sameness of life here. Thinking all this and wanting to scream—or get the hell out.

Or both.

As she passed the mirror in the entry hall, Freddie caught a glimpse of a woman of a certain age, the white shorts emphasizing her legs, her small feet sheathed not in high heels—that was too much—but in the more reserved but hopefully provocative kitten heels. That woman in the mirror didn't look so bad, but it struck Freddie that she was certainly no seductress.

Unsettled and nervous, she moved away, still uncertain about what she had come dressed for—or whether she had dressed for anything beyond a muggy Florida afternoon. A tryst? Was this a tryst? Before today she would have thought herself long past the time—or the age—of trysts; even using the word let alone participating in one.

From outside, she heard the sound of a motor and the crunch of gravel that signaled his arrival. Her stomach tightened. How should she position herself? Splayed out provocatively on the nearby sofa? No, that would be too much.

Then there was a knock on the door and that solved that. Whatever state she would have placed herself, she would still— as she did now—answer the door.

Resplendent—and that was the only word for him—in a freshly ironed untucked white linen shirt and artfully faded jeans, Dwight stood in the doorway leaning on his cane.

"There you are," Freddie said as if surprised that he was here.

"Can I come in?"

"Yes, please," she said, quickly stepping back from the door so that he could enter, trailing expensive cologne. Should she have dabbed on perfume? She'd never even thought of it.

Damn!

"You look nervous," he said, peering around.

"Do you think so? It's probably because I am nervous."

"This is your girlfriend's place?"

"I think she uses it basically as an income property, you know, vacation rentals, but yes, it's hers."

Dwight peered outside. "Nice view of the canal," he said vaguely.

"Yes." Freddie joined him studying the canal view.

"I should have brought something to drink," Dwight said.

"I never thought of it either," Freddie said. "I'm not much of a drinker."

"Me neither," Dwight said.

He took her in his arms. She stiffened. "Is this...?" he asked.

"Nervous, that's all."

He dropped his arms and pulled away from her. "Sorry..."

She watched him in some confusion. "Are you all right?"

"On the way over here, I was thinking about that weekend in New York."

"New York?" Freddie fought to recall any visit to New York with Dwight.

"What was supposed to be a wild romantic weekend. Do you remember that?"

"Yes." Freddie said vaguely.

"We stayed at The Pierre Hotel. They gave us this closet and the walls were so thin we could hear the couple in the room next door. And if we could hear them, then they could hear us and that certainly put a damper on things."

"They couldn't give us another room," Freddie said, having finally located that weekend in the far recesses of her memory bank.

"And then the next day, Saturday, it was pouring rain so we couldn't walk anywhere, and New York in the rain, cabs are impossible. Then Saturday night we saw the worst Broadway show I've ever seen in my life, before or since. And after that we couldn't get into a restaurant. I ended up furious. You were in tears. A disaster."

He flashed her a weak smile and shrugged. "That was pretty much the end of it, wasn't it?"

"I guess it was," Freddie said. The smile she flashed back at him was equally weak. "Is this the equivalent of that New York weekend?"

"Everything that's going on right now," Dwight said, moving away further. "Funny, I've thought about this so many times over the years. Now—now I just don't know if I'm ready...for this..."

Freddie wasn't sure whether to be shocked or relieved. Should she do something? Something seductive? But that was the last thing she desired—and from the look of Dwight, the last thing for him as well.

Then seduction became a moot point.

Two men in black burst in, their faces covered with ski masks. Freddie had an instant to register this before two more masked men, similarly dressed, barged through the front. Strong arms wrapped around her while a cloth was clamped against her face. A noxious smell assailed her nostrils and everything began to blur. She had a vague sense of Dwight being thrown to the floor.

And then there was nothing.

40

Two things struck Dwight McPhee when he regained consciousness. He was naked and he was in a low-ceilinged hellhole lit just enough to show the cinderblock walls. He was seated in a straight-back chair with arms. His hands were bound to the chair with zip ties. His ankles had been similarly bound to the legs of the chair.

Dwight had no sooner come to terms with his surroundings and his predicament when there was the sound of a heavy door banging open. A large black-bearded figure in a black track suit, wearing a black surgical mask, emerged out of the darkness. The big man stopped a few yards from where Dwight was seated. He put his hands on his hips.

"Mr. Dwight McPhee," the big man announced in a booming voice. "Welcome. You are in the presence of that most feared of all beings, a Russian gangster. Yes, we are a formidable breed, no question, totally ruthless, known to be willing to do anything to achieve our goals."

He moved closer to Dwight and continued, "Now if you were to inspect my body, which will not be allowed today, you would not find jailhouse tattoos, although you will have to take my word for that. The reason I do not have tattoos all over my body is very simple—I am a *smart* Russian gangster. Which is to say I have never ended up in prison.

"Because I am a Russian gangster, feared around the world I would say, and a *smart* Russian gangster to boot, you must do as I say. If you do not, I will kill you. I will do it very slowly, and because I am so damned smart, I will get away with it, as I have gotten away with many, many other terrible killings."

Dwight had to force himself to squeeze out a sentence. "What do you want?"

"Ah, yes, I must *want* something, am I right? Why would you be sitting here naked, tied to a chair, if I didn't want something?"

Dwight did not respond. The big man appeared momentarily impatient. "Mr. Dwight McPhee, please answer me. You are here because there is something I want. Is that not correct?"

Dwight nodded, "Yes…"

"Good. Then the question becomes what is it a tattooless Russian gangster would want? That is what I would like you to consider. What could I possibly *desire* that would make me go to such lengths to get it from you? Think about that for a while."

"I don't understand…" Dwight's words were even more choked.

"Naturally, you do not. This is all new to you. But give it some time and thought. What is it that I would want that only you could provide? *Think!*"

"Money?" Dwight called out, his voice echoing in the darkened room.

But the big man had already disappeared.

Sometime later, Dwight again heard the sound of the heavy door slamming open. Although he was similarly dressed in black, and wearing the same type of black mask, this was not the big man but a tall scarecrow. The scarecrow man strode with great confidence to Dwight and backhanded him hard across the face.

The stinging blow sent Dwight rocking back in his chair. The scarecrow man righted the chair before it could topple over. "The other guy?" the scarecrow man said. "That other guy was the *pussy* guy. I am no pussy I can tell you. I am the real, nasty shit. That pussy will threaten you. Me? I will *kill* you—and smile while I am doing it."

The scarecrow man leaned over to place his large hands on either side of Dwight's face, squeezing, forcing Dwight's head up so that he was staring into pits-of-hell eyes exposed by the mask. "What's it going to be, asshole? Are you going to tell me what I want to hear?"

"Money…" Dwight managed to gurgle.

The scarecrow man responded with another sharp blow. "*Money?*" He shouted the word, his masked face inches from Dwight's. "You got it right. *Money!* Lots of it."

He drew away from Dwight, breathing hard. "Now, tell me what we want lots of money in exchange for. Tell me that."

Dwight looked at the scarecrow man with a puzzled expression. "Me?" he ventured.

The scarecrow man backhanded Dwight again. "Wrong answer, you worthless prick. Who gives a shit about *you?*"

"What?" Dwight managed. "What do you want?"

"Your *daughter*, asshole. Becky McPhee, the missing astronaut you've been hiding away. The end of the world, right? Except it's not the end of the world; it's the end of the game you've been playing with the world. That's what it is."

"What…what are you talking about?" Dwight was leaning forward spitting blood from his cut lip.

"We've got her, she is ours." The scarecrow man was leaning over Dwight.

"That's…impossible." Dwight's head had jerked up, his face full of confusion."

"You think so? You think I can't do whatever the hell I set out to do?"

The scarecrow man struck again, so hard this time it sent Dwight's chair toppling back onto the concrete floor. He cried out, anguished, weeping.

"I should kill you right now, you bastard!" The scarecrow man stood over Dwight in a rage, fists clenched.

Dimly, Dwight heard the crash of the door opening and someone shouting, "Hey, that is enough!"

The big man swam into view, pushing away the scarecrow man. "What are you doing?" he demanded. "What the hell do you think you are doing?"

"Getting ready to kill the bastard. What do you think I'm doing?" The scarecrow man seethed with anger.

"You're not killing anyone," the big man said. "Get the hell out, let me handle this."

"You are soft, too easy on him," the scarecrow man said.

"Get out," ordered the big man. "Get the hell out!"

The big man lifted Dwight off the floor and righted him in the chair. Dwight slumped forward trying to breathe, spitting more blood.

"I apologize for my colleague," the big man said. "He is a violent, troubled soul. We never should have let him near you."

"My daughter… he was talking about my daughter."

"I asked you before, Mr. Dwight McPhee, what is it we would want from you."

"Money…the other fellow said money…"

"Yes, money would help matters certainly…"

"My daughter…do you have my daughter or not?"

"Unfortunately, that is the case, yes."

"But that can't be…"

"In life, what cannot be has a way of becoming what is. Particularly when you are dealing with hard, resourceful men such as ourselves."

"No…"

"Not to worry so much. Becky is okay—at least for the time being." The big man spoke reassuringly. "I will make sure that no harm comes to her. You have my word. In the meantime, I would like you to do some more thinking about the subject of money. So necessary, this money. Life. Death. It all comes down to money, do you not agree? Money provides life. In its absence, death looms before us."

Dwight hung his head, blood dripping from his mouth.

"Now I would like you to consider how much it is worth for us to reunite you with your Becky. If we can agree to a mutually acceptable sum, we will release the two of you, and then we will all remain quiet. We will also keep to ourselves the dirty little secret shared by you and your daughter."

"Secret…?" Dwight looked even more puzzled.

"Listen, do not be concerned. You are among bad people who don't care what you have been trying to pull off. We would even applaud your actions. After all, we too are criminals."

Dwight stared at him uncomprehendingly.

"This can all be resolved to everyone's satisfaction. Again, I make apologies for the violence of my colleague. Unnecessary. Except, I suppose, it does give you an idea of what awaits should you decline to cooperate."

"What about Fredryka?"

"Fredryka is safe."

"Will you release her as well?"

"Naturally. You see how amenable we are? Notwithstanding my colleague, we have no desire to hurt anyone."

"I want…to cooperate," Dwight said, slurring his words through the blood in his mouth. "We can work this out…it's possible…"

"Ah," said the big man. "I thought so. When there is cooperation, everything is possible."

"How much do you want?"

"I must first speak to my colleagues. After that, I return with a suitable figure."

Then the big man was gone. Dwight leaned forward, the enveloping silence broken by the sound of his breathing and his blood splattering on the concrete floor.

And something else.

A distant pop. And then another.

Then more pops.

Dwight lifted his head.

Gunshots…

41

As soon as the sound of the gunshots ceased, Dwight heard the familiar bang that was the door opening. His stomach fell as the fear rose. They were coming for him!

Instead, Freddie darted into view. Dwight blinked, hardly believing what he was seeing through the haze of his pain.

"Dwight," Freddie said anxiously.

Dwight tried to say something but the words wouldn't come out, and besides, by this time, there was someone else in the room. Tree Callister looked a whole lot less concerned than his wife.

As Freddie worked on the zip ties binding him, a red-headed woman appeared. She looked much meaner than Freddie. The gun she was holding helped with the meanness.

The red-headed woman with the gun took one look at Dwight and said, "We've got Freddie. What the hell? After what he's done, leave him,"

"My daughter." The words exploded out in a rush. "We've got to help my daughter..."

Tree looked at him. "What's this about your daughter?"

"They kidnapped her!"

"Miranda?" Tree asked. "Why would they kidnap her?"

"Not Miranda—Becky..."

Dwight's three rescuers exchanged quick glances. "There's no one else here," Gladys said. "Just the two of you. The people holding you have taken off—for now. I have to say pal, we're here for Freddie, not you. We take you with us and you're a liability."

"Dwight comes with us," Freddie said insistently. She got his wrists free and then kneeled to work on his ankles.

"Please," Dwight said pleadingly. "The Kremlin people promised..."

"The Kremlin people?" Tree said. "what are you talking about?"

"Get me out of here. I'll explain everything."

The leg restraints came loose. Freddie helped Dwight to his feet. He looked down at himself in shock. "Jesus, I've got no clothes on."

Gladys pointed with her gun. "They're in the corner. If we're taking this jerk with us, we've got to get moving. He can dress in the truck."

With Freddie helping, they moved Dwight to the rear where there was a door. Gladys pushed it open and they all went out onto a loading dock. It was pouring rain. Gladys's truck was parked below the dock.

Dwight held onto his clothes for dear life as Tree helped him get seated in the back and then squeezed in beside him. Freddie got into the front with Gladys behind the wheel starting the engine.

"Let's go," Gladys said.

———————

"How did you know where to find us?" Dwight asked. He was struggling into his clothes as he talked. Gladys was bent over the wheel, peering intently into pelting rain.

"I'd like to know, too," Freddie said.

When Tree failed to answer, Gladys filled in: "I believe what Tree doesn't know quite how to tell you, Freddie, is that he was suspicious about you and Dwight. He followed you to the house by the canal. Have I got that right, Tree?"

"Yes, that's about right."

"After Dwight arrived, Tree wasn't sure what to do. Then, who should show up but bad guys with guns wearing ski masks. Tree had the wherewithal to follow them to that warehouse complex we just left. On the way, he called in the cavalry—me."

"But how did you—those were pretty tough characters," Dwight said. "They bragged to me how tough and ruthless they are."

"Words don't count," Gladys said. "They're only Russian mean. I'm American mean. American mean trumps Russian mean every time."

Dwight turned to Tree. "I want you to know, Tree, that whatever you may think, nothing happened between Freddie and myself. Neither of us wanted to be anything more than old friends."

"You were going to tell us about the people who have Becky," Tree said.

"Which sounds like a bunch of BS to me," offered Gladys from behind the wheel.

"It's not," snapped Dwight. "It sounds crazy, I know. But it's all real. They're determined to disrupt everything, that's what it's all about. They wanted to tear this country apart, I tell you."

Tree said, "Kremlin people... you mean Russian intelligence agents?"

Dwight nodded. "The same people who disrupted American elections. Who sabotaged an electrical grid in Texas. Who tell you vaccines don't work. All part of their vast disinformation campaign. If I didn't believe any of it before, I believe it now."

"Abducting Becky was part of that?"

"An expansion of the disinformation campaign that they have been orchestrating for years. In this case, you make it so an American heroine disappears. The whole country is thrown into chaos. Everybody questions everything even more than before. The perfect doomsday scenario."

"But Dwight," Tree interjected, "from the look of things, you participated in all this, cooperated with them."

"It's the same as what happened tonight," Dwight replied. "You are forced into a situation that leaves you with no choice." Dwight shook his head sadly. "Listen, I'm really worried about my daughter. Those people back there, they said they have her."

"She wasn't with them at the warehouse," Tree said. "It looks as if they were lying in order to extort money from you."

"I must be sure." Dwight sounded desperate. "I'm begging you to take me to her. Then I'll know for sure that she's safe."

"Do you know where Becky is?"

Dwight hesitated and then lowered his head and said, "Yes."

42

Gladys drove through an open gate shrouded in haze. The rain had mostly stopped by the time she parked. The heat of the night closed in. Tree expected security guards to challenge their arrival. But as they got out, there was no one.

Suddenly, the area was bathed in harsh white light from a battery of LED security lights. Everyone froze.

"What the hell?" murmured Gladys. Tree noticed that Gladys had drawn her gun.

The three sliding doors in the nearby garage began to rise, reminding Tree of a metallic robot slowly opening its trio of eyes. Judy was outlined in the light from inside the garage. The ascending doors on either side of her revealed the missing security guards. They were clad in black to match their Kevlar vests and automatic weapons.

"Nothing's changed, Tree," Judy called. "I still don't want you at my house."

"Becky," Dwight blurted. "I need to see her."

"You're a gullible jackass, Dwight," Judy said. "You shouldn't have come—and you should never have brought these idiots with you."

"Becky's here with you, Judy," Tree said. "You've been hiding her."

"I haven't the faintest idea what you're talking about."

"Dwight has told us most of what went on," Tree said. "The Kremlin would have needed someone in this country who could be trusted and who could help them with their disinformation schemes. I should have realized that you would be the perfect candidate, Judy. Anything to stay on Putin's good side, I would guess."

"Please," Dwight cried out. "I need to know Becky's safe."

Judy said, "Don't you get it, Dwight? They have duped you to get you to talk. You're a fool."

Clint Stark and Chip Holbrook came out of the garage cradling their weapons, moving to Dwight. "Hey, there, Mr. McPhee, we're going to take you home."

Beside Tree, Gladys grew tense. "It's okay, Gladys," Tree murmured. "Let it go."

"Bastards," she hissed.

"Yes," Dwight said distractedly. "I should go home. I shouldn't be here."

Clint viewed Tree through the narrowed slits of his eyes. He and Chip flanked a broken, confused Dwight, leading him back to Judy.

"That's it," Judy called to Tree. "I don't know what you've tried to pull off—I'm sure Dwight will fill me in. But it didn't work. It never does with you, does it? You screwed up again. Par for the course."

"I can understand your thinking, Judy," Tree said. "You do what's necessary to remain Putin's American pal, no matter how crazy the demands they make of you. What I don't understand is how you convinced Becky and her father to go along with this hairbrained scheme."

"Get the hell off my property, Tree," Judy called.

Tree glanced at Gladys, strung tight, like a gunfighter at the showdown, and for a second or two, he feared what she might do. But then she took a deep breath and began backing away.

"I'll get the truck started," she said.

Tree took Freddie's arm. "Let's get out of here."

"What a good idea," Freddie said.

They went back down the drive and as they did, the LED security lights switched off. The garage doors began to lower. The darkness of the night took over.

Gladys was in the lead as they reached the truck. She went around to the driver's side, and abruptly stopped. "What's wrong?" Tree asked.

She pointed inside to where Becky McPhee was seated in the back. Tree stepped forward and opened the rear door.

"Please," Becky said to him. "I can't do this anymore. I can't be part of it. I have to get away."

"Part of what, Becky?" Tree asked.

"They used me. I'm not going to be used anymore."

"What do you want me to do?"

Freddie had moved forward to stand beside Tree

"Take me away from here, please, before they realize I'm gone."

43

ONE DAY BEFORE THE END OF THE WORLD

The press conference was scheduled for two o'clock at the Sanibel Community House, the day before the solar eclipse, the final day before the end of the world.

At one-thirty, a high wind blew across the island with rain forecast. The wind and the threatening rain failed to deter crowds gathered once again along Periwinkle Way. The press conference had attracted an even larger media presence, more big white trucks than ever jammed into the parking lot adjacent to the Community House and across the road.

Tree held the door for Becky as she climbed out of the Mercedes. Freddie followed. A roar went up from across the street. Becky ignored the clamor. She was dressed in an Eileen Fisher navy suit. Her face was clear. Her eyes sparkled. Even if she wasn't, she gave every appearance of being calm and composed. Tree took her by the arm and drew her to one side. "I'm not going to tell them everything," she said to him.

"That's fine," Tree said. "But you have to come clean with me before we go inside."

"What are you talking about?"

"Otherwise, I will tell the people in there what I know about the hoax you and your father along with Judy and her Russian friends have tried to pull off. What I don't know, and what you had better tell me right now, is why. Why did you and your father go along with this nonsense?"

"If I told you I didn't have any choice would that satisfy you?" Becky said quietly.

"That's what your father told me."

Becky hesitated, took a deep breath. "All right. Here's the story. He kept me in the dark, but my father had been doing badly in business. The McPhee Group not only was losing money but it was being investigated by the FBI. Clients were running for the doors. My dad desperately needed money to stay afloat, to be part of a Russian space company he had invested in heavily."

"RKK Energiya," Tree said.

"That's right," Becky said, showing surprise. "You know about it?"

"I know Judy is also an investor, not much else."

"Valentin introduced Judy to my father. Dad was convinced this was the way to pay off his debts and get back on his feet. In order to invest, though, he got mixed up with some pretty shady characters who turned out to be part of Russian organized crime. When RKK Energiya didn't pay off the way it was supposed to, those very bad people came after Dad, threatening his life. That's when he turned to Judy for help."

"And the price she demanded in exchange for protecting your father from the Russian mob was you disappearing."

"Let's say that's when Judy revealed herself to be much more ruthless than I would ever have imagined."

"Judy's people kidnapped you?"

"What I can say is, Russian security is very good when it comes to advice on who is professional enough to make a kidnapping look convincing."

"At the beach, you knew what was going to happen?"

"Let's say I accepted Judy's invitation to be her house guest for a time."

"And what about now?"

"My father and Judy are on their way to Moscow as we speak, supposedly to firm up his investment in RKK Energiya. If I say the right things at this press conference, then everything will be all right. My father will be safe. If I don't..." Becky allowed the sentence to trail off.

She gave Tree a look. "From the start, I've been trying to protect my father. That's what all this has been about, really."

"Yes," Tree said.

"I'm going to keep doing that, unless you decide differently." Her steely gaze was focused on him. "What about it, Tree? What are you going to do?"

"Make your speech," Tree said.

Her eyes softened. She squeezed his arm, and smiled. "I'm going to make you the hero."

"Don't bother," he said.

"No bother at all." She let go of his arm and started away.

He called to her: "Becky—"

She turned.

"Did you hear the Voice? Or was that Vladimir Putin?"

Becky opened her mouth to say something. Then she stopped.

And smiled.

———

Tree spotted Special Agent Drew Castle getting out of an SUV. Two other agents were with her. Freddie joined Becky moving toward the rear entrance as Drew approached Tree. He thought about what he had just heard from Becky; thought about what he should say to the FBI agents.

Drew did not look happy, but then Tree had long since

grown used to the large number of law enforcement officers who did not look happy when he was around.

"What do you think you're up to?" she demanded.

"I'm here for Becky's press conference like everyone else."

"We're looking for Judy Markov," Drew said. "Any idea where we can find her?"

"Judy doesn't keep in touch with me," Tree answered—which was more or less true.

"And what of Dwight McPhee?"

"What about him?"

"We'd also like to talk to him, but he seems to have conveniently disappeared along with Mrs. Markov. Do you know anything about that?"

"Not a thing," Tree said. "Right now, I have to get inside. Becky is about to make a statement."

"We're not finished with you, Callister," Drew said sternly. "And believe me when I say this is far from over."

"You have no idea how many members of the various arms of the police community over the years have told me the same thing."

"Yeah, well, I believe I previously mentioned that I'm not like other members of law enforcement."

"I'll keep that in mind," Tree said.

Tree turned and started for the rear entrance. He caught sight of Sanibel Detectives Cee Jay Boone and Owen Markfield. They did not look any happier than Special Agent Drew Castle.

Who could blame them?

And then there was Tommy Dobbs. He looked a lot happier than members of law enforcement, Tree thought. A tall, long-limbed beauty with high cheekbones and full lips held tightly to Tommy's hand.

"There you are, Mr. Callister," he said.

"Here I am Tommy," Tree said.

"Thomas, Mr. Callister. I wanted to introduce you to my friend, Daria Kotova. She is a producer at RTRN, that's the Russian broadcasting network."

"My friends call me Cat," Daria said.

"Kotova means cat in Russian," Tommy added helpfully.

"Nice to meet you, Cat," Tree said.

"You wanted me to find out who asked Becky a question in Russian," Tommy said. "Well, I found out." He gave Daria an affectionate look. She returned it and squeezed his hand.

"What did you ask Becky?"

Daria smiled and said, "I ask her if she had a favorite dish to prepare over the next ten days."

"Becky said she would have to think about that," Tommy added.

Aha, Tree thought. Mystery solved.

44

Freddie and Becky waited in the kitchen as Tree entered. Gladys was there, too, leaning against the sink with her arms folded. From inside her jacket, Becky removed the copy of the statement she planned to read.

"All set?" Tree asked.

She nodded and straightened her shoulders as though preparing for a blow. Then she pushed open the swinging kitchen door and strode in to face the waiting reporters and cameras.

The room fell silent as Becky stepped behind the podium that had been set up for her. Not far away, Tree and Freddie, as well as Gladys, stationed themselves along the wall. Tree spotted Tommy Dobbs with his new friend Daria—or Cat—among the seated press. He gave Tree a wave. Daria waved too.

"Good afternoon, ladies and gentleman," Becky said into the microphone. "Can everyone hear me all right?"

Following a murmur of assent, Becky, sounding strong and authoritative, began reading her statement.

"Many of you have been concerned over the past days as to my whereabouts. I wish to apologize to you all this afternoon. Returning from the challenges of being in space for the first time, hearing something that had a life-changing effect on me, and then returning to earth and the ensuing controversy inadvertently caused by my statements, I simply panicked and felt I had to get away—to hide from everything and try to come to terms with what I had heard and what I had, as I say, accidentally unleashed. I'm back today because I've come to realize that, as someone else said, it's okay not to be okay.

"I have not been okay lately. But I am here today to tell you that I am much better.

"I'm afraid I used one of the members of my security team, Mr. Tree Callister, to make my exit. I know Mr. Callister was attacked on the beach after I left him, but that attack had nothing to do with me. I had already walked away and entered the beach parking area when the assault occurred. I was unaware of what happened. Mr. Callister has been unfairly accused of somehow being involved in a plot to kidnap me. I was not kidnapped and certainly Mr. Callister had nothing to do with it.

"In fact, in their untiring efforts to find me and bring me back safely, Mr. Callister, his wife, Fredryka and their associate, Gladys Demchuk, have shown extraordinary patience and sensitivity. Thanks to Tree"—and here she glanced over at Tree against the wall—"I came to realize that it would be in everyone's best interest if I clarified my previous statements. He convinced me that it really is okay not to be okay and to speak my truth.

"And the truth is, yes, no matter what anyone may think, I did hear that voice, but I must tell you that I don't believe the world will end today or with tomorrow's solar eclipse or the day after that. We have all been through a great deal these past few years, but we will all survive and so will the world. Thanks to Mr. Tree Callister, I know the world is still very much here and what is more, it is full of kind and caring and compassionate people."

Becky's eyes filled with tears as she returned her gaze to Tree. "In fact, as far as I'm concerned, Tree Callister has saved the world—he most certainly saved *my* world."

She wiped the tears from her eyes as she refocused on the now stirring press crowd. "Anyway, that's it. That is all I have to say. That is all I will say. I am moving on with the rest of my life. Thank you all for being here."

Becky gathered up her statement and amid a cacophony of shouted questions, she hurried away through the kitchen door.

Tree came out in time to see her climbing into an SUV. He caught a glimpse of Miranda McPhee at the wheel as the SUV swept past. Was that Miranda giving him the finger just before she veered onto Periwinkle and sped away?

Yes, Tree concluded, yes it was.

Then Tree was engulfed by a swarm of reporters and cameramen. Dimly, he heard Tommy Dobbs calling, "Mr. Callister… Mr. Callister—how does it feel to have saved the world…?"

———————

Freddie finally managed to pull Tree away from Tommy and the rest of the press throng shouting insistently for more answers than either he or Becky had provided.

Inside the Mercedes it was abruptly eerily quiet. Freddie drove onto Periwinkle Way toward Captiva, the traffic held back by frantically waving sheriff's deputies.

As she drove, Freddie got her breathing under control again and then shot a glance at Tree. "Well, that was something, wasn't it? But you know what?"

"What?"

"I don't think you're telling me everything."

"The FBI appears to think the same thing."

"Except I'm not the FBI. What did Becky tell you outside?"

"She said she was going to make me a hero."

"Which she did."

"It's a bright, sunny afternoon in Florida and the world hasn't come to an end at least so far," Tree observed.

"Don't tell me. Because you saved it."

"You know me. Despite my monumental achievement, I plan to remain the same humble, lovable guy I've always been."

"Heaven help us all." Freddie shook her head. "The Sanibel Sunset Detective saves the world."

Tree kept his eyes on the road as he said, "We haven't talked about Dwight."

"Aha, I wondered when that subject would come up," Freddie said.

"I thought I'd wait until after the world was saved—just in case."

"What about Dwight?" Freddie asked.

"How you felt being with him."

"You mean coming on to him and playing the role of the femme fatale at my age?"

"You've always been the femme fatale as far as I'm concerned."

"First of all," Freddie said. "I had my doubts that I could even get away with it, given my age…"

"For what it's worth, I had no doubts at all," Tree said.

"And then, although I went along with your plan, I can't say I felt very good about it on a number of levels, the morality of it, the idea of being the goat staked out at the watering hole…"

"I'm sorry about that," Tree said. "I thought it was necessary."

"Except you knew, didn't you?"

"Knew what?"

"You knew where Becky was."

"I suspected," Tree countered. "I wasn't sure until Dwight led us to Judy's place. No way could we have gotten there without him, and he would never have taken us in if we hadn't put on that show with the assistance of Georgi and Nino and Nino's henchmen."

"All in the name of saving mankind," Freddie said wryly.

"Don't tell anyone, but I have a feeling mankind would have survived just fine without us," Tree said.

"With all its imperfections."

"Even with all its imperfections," Tree agreed.

45

THE END OF THE WORLD

Good news," announced Rex Baxter, speaking over the din of afternoon patrons at tables lined along the deck of the Bimini Bait Shack. The restaurant was packed, everyone anxious to witness the rare total solar eclipse that would mark the beginning of the end of the world.

"The world isn't coming to an end?" suggested Gladys.

"Even better," said Rex. "My agent has sold the movie rights to my novel. Netflix is adapting it. They're turning my life into what it always should have been, a movie."

"You're finally going to be a star," Tree said.

"I would argue that I have always been a star," Rex said. "It's just that Hollywood didn't realize it until now."

"That's wonderful news, Rex," Freddie enthused. "It's a terrific book and it will make a wonderful film."

"What's more, all of a sudden my publisher is showing a whole lot more interest in the book. They're launching a new marketing campaign. The angle for press interviews is not only the Netflix movie but also that I've known Tree since he was a young man. I can provide the inside scoop on the private detective who saved the world."

"Rex, I did not save the world," Tree protested.

"What difference does that make? I'm trying to sell a book here. The promotional approach is that I had no idea that someday you *would* save the world."

"You're too modest, Tree," Gladys said with a wry smile. She was standing at the railing with Tree, Freddie, and Rex. "But then you heroes always are, aren't you?"

"Tree is so modest," Freddie joined in with an equally wry smile. "Saving the world hasn't changed him in the least."

"Yeah, well, we will know for sure in a few minutes whether the world has been saved or not," Rex said. "For the sake of my future in Hollywood, let's hope it has."

It began to grow dark. A murmur of excitement went through the onlookers. "Here we go," Rex said. They put on the special eclipse glasses Gladys had purchased for the occasion.

The sky above San Carlos Bay turned blacker. The buzz of excitement rose. Despite himself, despite everything he had told himself, everything Becky had said, Tree nonetheless grew more nervous. He gripped Freddie's hand.

"There, there," she cooed. "It's going to be all right."

"You are much more of an optimist than I am," Tree said.

Then, seemingly out of nowhere, a dark thunderhead filled the sky, obscuring the sun. A couple of minutes later, rain poured down in sheets. Amid loud groans of disappointment, everyone on the deck hurriedly retreated inside the restaurant. Meanwhile, as the rain came down, day was turned into night.

"It's happening," Gladys said. "Even though we can't see it, the eclipse is happening."

The thudding rain, accompanied by explosions of thunder, continued as, minutes later, the world began to lighten again.

"Well, we're all still here," stated Rex.

Loud thunder shook the Bait Shack. Fierce forks of lightning lit the sky. For a time, it looked as though it might in fact be the end of the world.

But then the thunder drifted off, the echo of artillery fire fading. There was no more lightning as the rain let up, the day hurrying to be just another day. A cheer went up inside the Bait Shack. Relief? Tree wondered. On the sound system Jimmy Buffet sang "Trip Around the Sun," Jimmy hanging on while "this old world keeps spinning." The fish tank bar swarmed with customers ordering nerve-settling drinks. Freddie suddenly embraced her husband. "Maybe you did save the world after all," she said.

Gladys wiped away a tear.

"Gladys," Tree said in surprise.

"Well, shit, you never know," she said. "Goddamn, some days it's good to be alive." She embraced an equally surprised Rex.

Gladys let go of Rex and turned to Tree. "You know, the thing we still have to deal with is the possibility that Becky McPhee really did hear a voice in space. Maybe she just got the date wrong."

"And certainly no one was expecting another total eclipse so soon after the one in 2017," Freddie added.

"But nonetheless, nothing happened," Rex said. "We're all still here."

"Nothing has happened *yet*," Freddie said. "Maybe what Becky heard was a warning that we'd better smarten up and pay more attention to making the world better if we want it to go on spinning."

"There you go, Tree," Rex said. "You'd best stand by. You may be called on to save the world again."

"I'm willing to do everything I can," Tree said. He put his arm around Freddie. "But saving the world this first time has tired me out."

"Then let's go home," Freddie said, hugging him.

46

The air was muggy and oppressive as they arrived back at Andy Rosse Lane. The sun had managed to shake itself free from obscuring clouds to shine uncertainly through rising heat waves.

As soon as they were inside, Freddie wrapped her arms around Tree's neck and said, "Do you know what I would like?"

"Anything," Tree pronounced. "Anything, you like."

"I would like to make love with the man who saved the world."

Tree frowned. "I don't think that will be possible."

"No? I'm really disappointed to hear that."

"However, if you'd like to have sex with Tree Callister... well then..."

"You?" Freddie kissed him softly on the mouth. "Well, yes, now that I think about it, I believe you will do..."

She kissed him some more.

The sound awoke Tree.

At least, he thought there was a sound. Freddie slept on soundlessly with her back to him. He looked at his watch. It was 2:30 in the morning. He lay on his back for a few minutes wondering if he was hearing things.

Uneasy now, feeling anxious, thinking that, yes, the world was still here and he was alive in it having lately made love to the most beautiful, wonderful woman in that surviving world.

But still, how long could that last? How much longer could *he* last? After all, the world most likely would go on, but he wouldn't. Any way you looked at it, this was his third act; he was much closer to the end, as he kept telling himself, than he was to the beginning.

And every day brought him that much closer to the end.

His anxiety beginning to overwhelm him, Tree slipped out of bed. Dressed in a T-shirt and shorts, he grabbed his cellphone and padded barefoot outside onto Andy Rosse Lane, taking deep breaths from the muggy air, trying to settle his thumping heart. The rain had turned the pavement into a glistening black strip stretching toward the beach. The moon, after swallowing the sun that day, hung fat and complacent over the palm trees.

To his surprise, his cellphone began making sounds. He looked at the screen, not recognizing the number.

"I hear you're the hero who saved the world." Judy Markov's voice crackled a bit, but otherwise came through loud and clear.

"You and I both know I'm not and I didn't."

"Nonetheless, I was impressed by how Becky handled explaining it all, very convincing. And since you're the hero of the moment, I guess Becky has persuaded you not to say anything."

"Is that why you're calling? To make sure I keep my mouth shut?"

"I'm in Moscow. Putting the finishing touches to this deal. Her father is going to be a very rich man."

"I can't believe you allowed yourself to be part of their scheme," Tree said.

"At the beginning I thought they were out of their minds," Judy said. "But it seems to have worked out to everyone's satisfaction. The Americans have their heroine. The Russians have their confusion. I have lots more money and so does Dwight McPhee. The world is still here. Why, it's even worked out for you, Tree. A win-win for everyone as they say."

"What do you think, Judy? This all started with a voice in space. Did Becky actually hear the Voice?"

"Tree, whatever your many shortcomings, you don't hear voices, at least not yet. Neither do I. But does someone else? Someone like Becky? Who knows?"

"I hate you for all this," Tree said.

"Sure, you do, Tree. Until the next time you need me."

"There won't be a next time."

That got a laugh out of Judy. "We'll see."

The line went dead.

Tree swallowed a couple of more times, making himself calm down. He put the phone away. He was suddenly very tired.

A figure came looping toward him from the direction of the beach, a familiar thin man in a bright Hawaiian shirt this early morning, his head topped by the same worn brown fedora. The man's dark, ravaged face brightened when he saw Tree. He slowed.

"Micah," Tree said.

"You got it, partner. Micah it is. You remember me, right? The guy who looks like Morgan Freeman."

"How could I forget?"

"Not so hard, partner. Plenty of folks have no trouble at all forgetting me. Even if I do look like old Morgan. How are you doing on this moonlit night? You look kind off shaken up."

"It's the look I get after I've talked to my ex-wife," Tree said.

"What brings you out at such a late hour?"

"Went for a walk at the beach," he said. "Like to do it at this time of night. Nice and quiet, no one around to bother you. Gives a fellow like myself a chance to think."

"It does at that," Tree said.

"That why you're out here, partner? Thinking?"

"Couldn't sleep," Tree said. "Thinking about what you said earlier."

"What'd I say, partner? Remind me."

"About not measuring up."

Micah's eyebrows jumped in the moonlight. "Hey, the way I hear it, you saved the world this week. I guess that's kind of measuring up, wouldn't you think?"

"Yeah, except you and I know I didn't save the world."

"World's still here, isn't it?" Micah shrugged. "You can take credit for it as much as anyone, I suppose."

Micah started ambling away. Tree, called after him. "Hey…"

Micah turned. "What is it, partner?"

"Tell me it's going to be all right."

Micah thought about this, paused in the moonlight. "Tell you what you should do," he said finally.

"What's that?" Tree said.

"Simple really. Act justly and love mercy. You do those two things, partner, nothing else matters, everything will be fine."

"Justice and mercy," Tree repeated.

"That's it, partner."

Micah turned and resumed walking. Tree watched until he disappeared into the darkness. Then he went back in the house and crawled into bed beside Freddie. She stirred and said, "Where were you?"

"Getting some advice."

"Advice? At this time of night?"

"Act justly and love mercy," Tree said.

"What?"

"That's what we need to do to save the world."

"How do you know that?" Freddie asked sleepily.

"A guy on the street just told me."

"Go to sleep, Tree."

Acknowledgements

If you are a writer, a worldwide pandemic leaves you with little choice but to do what writers are supposed to do and yet try to avoid—write!

In the past two years, hunkered down in Milton, Ontario, unable to travel or even go out to a movie, I've certainly gotten plenty of writing done. I've had time to complete two Sanibel Sunset Detective novels (including this one), a Milton mystery, as well as finish the first two installments for a new series of mysteries set at London's iconic Savoy Hotel, co-authored with my longtime friend, Prudence Emery, who actually worked at the Savoy for five years.

Outside the tiny bubble in which my wife Kathy and I have existed, the world has been thrown into chaos. Millions have died; millions more have been made ill. How does a writer writing what are designed as entertainments deal with this sweeping reality?

Well, as you hopefully now have read, I've dealt with it by sending poor Tree Callister out to save the world. Sort of. What else can a hero, even an unlikely one like Tree, do in a vulnerable time such as this?

One of the benefits of being a writer is that you are able to leave reality behind and jump through the looking glass into a world that you have created and where you are in control. That's been particularly true over these many months. I've been able to get away not only to Sanibel Island, Florida, but also to London, England and live in a legendary luxury hotel. I've even exercised control over my life in Milton, something I'm not otherwise able to do.

In order to keep pulling off these escapes, I've needed smart, knowledgeable accomplices. I have been exceedingly fortunate to be supported by a crack team dedicated to ensuring that I don't screw up—or screw up a lot less than I otherwise would. As I have said so many times, they work tirelessly to save me from myself, beginning with my wife Kathy Lenhoff, first reader (and often the last), best pal, and, most importantly, the love of my life.

Editors David Kendall, Alexandra Lenhoff and James Bryan Simpson took turns beating me up in an alley until the manuscript was in publishable shape. Brother Ric Base, as he has from the beginning of these books, oversaw production, while designer Jennifer Smith once again brought her talents to the task of creating the cover.

As I finished *The Sanibel Sunset Detective Saves the World*, I considered finally leaving Tree to fend for himself. After all, what do you do with a hero after he has saved the world? But then late the other night, as he usually does, Tree came calling. He has another adventure in store. What can I do but once more follow him through the looking glass, filled with curiosity about what he's going to get up to this time?

MURDER AT THE SAVOY

The time: 1968; the location: London's Savoy, the world's most famous and luxurious hotel.

Our unlikely heroine is Priscilla Tempest, the eager-to-please head of the Savoy Press Office, a young woman who adores champagne and becoming involved with the wrong men.

Currently, she has her hands full as the rich, famous, and aristocratic arrive from all over the world.

Elizabeth Taylor and Richard Burton are drinking too much champagne in the American Bar. The iconic American comedian Bob Hope is making demands as he is about to hold a press conference. Singer Liza Minnelli wants to make a very important announcement. Luciano Pavarotti is fast becoming a legend next door at the Royal Opera House. The playwright Noël Coward is forever looking for someone to share a Buck's Fizz.

And...?

Well, there is the matter of the dead body in river suite 705.

A dead body at the Savoy? Impossible! But there you have it. The dead man is a notorious international arms dealer named Amir Abrahim. What's uncertain is whether he was murdered. The police are baffled.

It soon is revealed that our Priscilla had been with Amir the night before he was found dead. This brings her under the suspicious gaze not only of Scotland Yard Inspector Robert "Charger" Lightfoot, but also of her boss, the Savoy's unforgiving general manager, Clive Banville.

And was that a notorious member of the Royal family seen leaving Amir's suite minutes before his body was discovered?

Suspected of murder, her job on the line, Priscilla had better get to the bottom of what happened in suite 705—and do it fast.

A plucky heroine! The world's most famous hotel! Swinging 1960s London in full swing! Lots of champagne! A bit of humor! And just possibly—

Murder at the Savoy!

Think *Fleabag* meets Agatha Christie. How can anyone possibly resist?

COMING SOON

THE SANIBEL SUNSET DETECTIVE GOES TO THE MOVIES

Tree Callister's best friend, Rex Baxter, has written a best-selling memoir. Now a Hollywood production company is on Sanibel Island shooting a movie based on the book. However, an unexpected twist has been added to the movie's plot—murder!

CPSIA information can be obtained
at www.ICGtesting.com
Printed in the USA
LVHW091943270821
696281LV00007B/473

9 781990 058011